The Last *Letter*

Author

A. A. Lewis

Printed in the United States of America

First Printing, 2021

D & S Publishing

5047 W. Main St, PMB 128

Kalamazoo, MI 49009

www.dspublishing.net

www.authoraalewis.com

Dedication- I dedicate this book to my loving husband- Darryl Lewis. I'm so glad to have you in my life.

I also would like to acknowledge those who every day wear the mask that shields their daily struggles. Mental illness is no laughing matter. And to the millions of individuals that suffer from some form of mental illness, know that you are not alone. I know all too well that you need the mask sometimes to hide behind the pretentious smile that you cover yourself with, and also the common phrases you disguise your tongue with just so that you can make it through the day. I want you to know that I see you, I hear you, and I understand.

If you or a loved one has a mental illness, struggles emotionally, or has concerns about their mental health, there are ways to gain assistance. Please use these resources to help find help for yourself, a friend or a family member.

National Suicide Hotline- 1-800-273-8255

Call 911

Crisis Text Line-Text HELLO to 741741

Veterans Crisis Line- 1-800-273 -8255

Disaster Distress Helpline- 1-800-985-5990 or text TALKWITHUS to 66746

For more information and educational programs, please contact the National Institute of Mental Health at www.NIMH.NIH.GOV

"What Mental health needs is more sunlight, more candor, and more unashamed conversation"

-Glenn Close

Today

There was an awkward silence that echoed in Tracy's head. She knew there was something that she should be doing. But there were no words nor activities that came to mind as she stood there in the now emptied house. The smell of Derrick's cologne welcomed her home, and the sight of his slippers at the door made everything seem so surreal. It was just hours before that he had asked her to dance with him and even joked about what their twenty-fifth anniversary would look like. The absence of noise surrounded Tracy as tears began to swell up in the corners of her eyes. "How could I not see the signs? How did I not know the pain Derrick was in? How could he.... Why did he... DAMN HIM!" she screamed, opening a floodgate of emotions that had all bottled up inside her.

Tracy sat on the love seat in the living room, feeling numb. The sounds of the birds outside mimicked the cheerfulness she was missing. It had been hours since she left the hospital and was denied access to the one person she had loved entirely. It had been hours since she waited outside in her car for an update on her husband. She watched as medical personnel covered in ill-fitted plastic garments, all wearing some kind of protective mask and latex gloves. They greeted the ambulances and cars that pulled in and out of the emergency room parking entrance, the same way that they greeted her. The hospital was on lockdown due to Covid-19, and only patients were being admitted, with others being given a correlating number to the patient they were waiting for or directed to the waiting area parking lot.

It all played out like a movie she once watched. Except for this time, the happy ending forgot to play out in her favor. Tracy just sat there, replaying the events of the day, trying to make sense of it all and then figure out how she ended up being there, and alone. If you had told her life would take such a drastic turn, she wouldn't believe you. She couldn't believe you. Derrick and Tracy were the couples' everyone wanted to be. They were college sweethearts, successful, and in love. Derrick had adorned Tracy with everything she had wanted and more. The way he looked at her made her feel like she was the only woman in the room and by far the prettiest. They had a love other's admired, and there was never a time that their behavior showed anything but the ideal marriage. But Tracy now knew that was a lie. A lie she had force fed herself and actively eaten daily. It was her own misguided understanding that she and Derrick controlled a situation and hidden his imperfections away from the world's view, until now. Until today, Tracy thought. Until the nurse rushed over to her parked vehicle, Tracy could see her face even with the mask on. Her face had the expression of panic and heartache. It leads Tracy to grab the non-surgical mask and place it on as the nurse approached the car. Tracy followed quickly behind her. She left her purse in the car and only managed to grab her keys.

The pounding of Tracy's heart played like the bass to her husband's favorite afro beat. Down the halls of Borgess Hospital, Tracy was lead.

She walks past the security check points and medical staff that were covered in their combat attire. She could hear the doctor's murmurs through their homemade mask as the nurse grabbed her hand and pushed through the last remaining doors. After what seemed like a maze of hallways and locked doors, she had finally arrived at her destination. When they say the eyes are the windows to the soul, nothing could be truer, as the apologetic stares glared back at her just as she was ushered into a small room. There lay Derrick. He was attached to several machines and tubes as the beat of his failing heart registered on the instruments' graphics monitoring him. She stood there. Tracy wanted to touch him. She wanted to call out his name but wondered if it would be in vain. She wanted to tell him that there was nothing she would not give to have him hold her one last time. Tracy wanted to say and do many things in that moment, but she could do nothing.

Her trance was broken only by the team of doctors that entered the small single patient size room. They were all wearing masks that covered their noses and mouths. But it was their eyes, their windows to their souls that spoke to me first. It was at that moment that she knew. Before words were ever spoken, she knew. Tracy looked back at Derrick. His still body, the calmness that resonated from him, and the inner peace his half smile gave; she knew.

There were no words that could console her. Doctors had questions, and Tracy answered the best she could. Tracy had memorized all of Derrick's medicines, so she gave what information she could recall. She watched as they pulled the tubes away from her husband's lips, unplugged the machines, and disconnected the monitoring devices. It was the ending and yet the beginning of her understanding of the man she had loved all these years. As the tears slowly flowed, she reluctantly signed document after document. Tracy watched as Derrick Allen Montgomery lay at peace for the first time in a long time, maybe ever in his life.

This Is The story of Derrick and Tracy Montgomery.

The Past

The year was 2012, I was fresh out of high school and excited to be away from home. I had managed to get accepted into the top five universities that I had applied for. Then after careful consideration, I decided that Western Michigan University was the school for me. Now don't get me wrong, no one wakes up one day and says that WMU is the place to be. Truth be told, I did not even know Western Michigan University existed, let alone where it was located. I was following behind my high school sweetheart. He was a Basketball player and at that time was recruited by WMU to play for them. They were a smaller Division I team, so this meant that D'Markus Edwards would stand a chance of being the star player for the team and an even bigger NBA recruit.

D'Markus was a year ahead of me. I had been on the campus many times since he walked the campus. I had made plans to be there every other weekend. Me and my girls would make the seven-hour drive from Buffalo NY, to Kalamazoo, MI. D'Markus and his teammates would welcome us and the care packages that accompanied our visits. His friends and my girlfriends would hit it off and before long, we were partying and hanging out. And a few times, they even made their way back to Buffalo to hang out with us on the weekends when we couldn't travel to Michigan.

It wasn't until I eventually started attending WMU that problems in my relationship with D'Markus began surfacing. I noticed that every other weekend gave D'Markus all the freedom he needed to mess around with other girls. Not that I thought he would be faithful, but I did believe he would at least have the common sense to wear a rubber. But now, all he seemed to do was lie to me. He started lying about unnecessary stuff. Plus, anytime a man starts the sentence off with "now see what had happened was" leads me to believe that the D'Markus I was in love with no longer existed outside of high school and what memories I had of us.

With D'Markus' newfound fame came the campus basketball fans' attention, which wasn't a surprise to me. But there was one fan in particular that I had ran into once too many times, Candice Walker. It seemed that Candice Walker knew how to do two things very well. She was your classic around the way hood girl. You know, the one that wears everything tight and leaves nothing to the imagination. Weave ponytail down her back and always popping gum like a cow. Despite her tacky clothing or the way she chewed that gum, Candice was intelligent. As D'Markus' math tutor, she helped him maintain a steady B average in that class. But what I did not know was that her tutoring skills also came with a side of ass. One would have thought she would have gotten more than good grades with all the time she spent on her knees. Hell, even with my skills, I at least collect valuables for my good deeds.

That was the first time I had my heart broken, but clearly, it would not be the last. I remember it like it was yesterday. I was walking back from my Theater Class after finding out it had been cancelled. The three-hour class anchored my Monday and Wednesday nights. I usually did not make it back to my dorm until just past 9:30 pm. But it was well worth the time. I had always had a fascination with acting. In fact, I was surprisingly good at it. I had done some small acting gigs as a child, and even starred in some community plays. My mother would say, "a pretty face will only get you so far." That was my mother's way of making sure I focused more on my books just as much as I did on boys. I majored in Business Management with a minor in Theatre Arts.

I had decided to head over to D'Markus' dorm room earlier than usual. I had stopped and picked up some tacos from the on-campus food truck that we all loved. It was his favorite late-night snack. I arrived at his complex and entered the door to the quad suite. He shared his suite with three of his basketball teammates, James and Walter, who were busy playing Madden On the X-Box. I waved and signaled the arrival of tacos. Without missing a beat, both in unison said thanks sis, and kept playing the game. I blew them kisses as I turned the handle to D'Markus' bedroom. There he sat on the edge of the bed, legs open, clutching the fake ponytail of Candice's bobbing head, while she swallowed his manhood. I wasn't sure if I saw this correctly, but after I blinked a few times, I focused on the way he coaxed her head into him, the same way he had done me. Even his moans mimicked the sounds I thought were reserved only for me. There he was, enjoying her skills, until the cold draft from the common area broke his focus; only then had he noticed me standing there.

Without saying a word, I got the fuck out of there. The tears rolled down my face as I ran across the large college campus. All I could think about was what a fool I had been. I gave up going to NYU to be with D'Markus. All the promises he made to me. All the times I looked at him through the rose colored glasses, excusing his flaws, had now come back to haunt me. I wasn't just mad at D'Markus, but I was mad at myself. I could hear D'Markus calling after me from a distance. I just kept on running. Not once did I look back. The tears lit my way back to my dorm. For the first time, my heart had broken and I understood the power of love and the pain that followed.

Weeks went by, and D'Markus tried like crazy to get me to talk to him. He made so many sorry attempts to apologize. He played Jodeci outside my dorm window. He stood outside my classes, begging for me to talk to him. He even sent me three dozen pink roses, but nothing eased my broken heart. I was mad cool with his boys, but when they came by trying to plead his case, I had to cut them off as well. The image of the two of them haunted my dreams for weeks, and no amount of sorry ass gifts was ever going to undo what I had seen.

One day while leaving my Wednesday night theater class, D'Markus was waiting outside. I saw him at the door and slid out the back entrance of the class. I figured it would take a few minutes before he would notice I wasn't coming out. I walked at a steady pace hoping to make it back to my dorm before he had the chance to catch up with me. I must have been deep in thought because I accidentally ran into a brick wall. No, not literally a brick wall, but he might as well had been one. There he stood about "6'3" 220lbs of muscle. It was his dimples that greeted me first.

"Hey shorty, you ok?" he asked.

I was dazed and mesmerized. Until now, I had only had eyes for D'Markus and with those rose-colored glasses broken, I was starting to see things just fine. In fact, I was back to 20/20 vision.

"Here, let me help you with that" the handsome stranger gestured, reaching for my hand as he helped me up from the ground. I could hear D'Markus calling after me in the near distance. I smiled at the stranger and tried to rush off. He noticed the look on my face and could sense my urgent need to flee, but he held my hand, and without a word, a sense of calmness came over me. D'Markus had managed to catch up to the stranger and I. There was an awkward silence that cascaded over us. The stranger was still holding on to me, then he looked at me and smiled. D'Markus had a puzzled look on his face at the intimate gesture that was taking place between my unnamed hero and myself.

''What the fuck is this Tracy?'' D'Markus demanded an answer.

"You don't have any right to ask me anything" I replied.

The stranger smiled; still holding me as he asked, "Tracy, is this guy bothering you?"

I looked at him amused. First, he was holding on to me and now he was going to defend my honor. If the dimples did not have me, this surely was making me wonder who this guy was. I shook my head as if to say no.

"What do you want D'Markus?" I questioned

"Baby I'm sorry, I mean, that bitch means nothing to me. It's you that I want to be with" he pleaded.

"D'Markus, the only thing you are sorry about is that you got caught." I spoke out loud.

"Tracy, baby that shit doesn't mean anything to me. I need you baby, I swear I'll never cheat on you, I'll never do it again!" D'Markus cried aloud.

I could see that he was hurting. I mean, why wouldn't he. I had been his rock and also the only constant in his life for so long. He had forgotten that. He had taken me for granted and now wished he had kept his empty promises and made good on his word. But it was too late. I was hurting just as much as he is, and the only difference was that I was putting my needs before his—something I had neglected to do many times in our past. I looked at him, and in that moment, this power forward who had managed to capture the hearts of WMU fans, who had a cult like following around town, who was the big man on campus, now seemed weak to me. Like a little boy who had lost his favorite toy. Well, I was no longer playing games. I wasn't his toy to toss and discard how he deems fit, and I damn sure wasn't going to put him first any longer.

D'Markus had motioned for me to come closer, but I took one step backward.

"D'Markus, we're done." I said as I turned and walked away. It was the opening chapter to the rest of my life. That night was the start of something new. I wasn't sure what it meant, but walking away from D'Markus, I was sure it was the best thing I had ever done. Even as I walked away, D'Markus never ran after me. I had reasoned because he forgot how to. You see, all the while in our relationship, I was the one chasing after him.

D'Markus called after me as I walked past the stranger who reminded me I was courageous. It was his eyes this time that lifted me and gave me a sense of empowerment. It was his dimples that melted away all the hurt I had been carrying around the past few weeks. I had fallen and managed to get back up figuratively and literally. It was the end and the beginning of how I would see love for my future self. I knew I did not want a selfish one-sided kind of love, like that I shared with D'Markus. I knew I did not want to lose myself in the process. So whatever love had in store for me was closer than I could imagine, and Mister Dimples felt it too.

The Present

I sat there in Derrick's office, packing up his belongings. I had always enjoyed visiting him at work. For many of his colleagues, Derrick and I was their first look into what a black couple should look like. I also like to think that we dispelled any negative notion on social media, the news, TV, or movies. We were the epitome of black royalty to many. I was the belle on his arm at work functions. I would work in the room and give a good presentation for my husband. I put those acting skills to work, and I mingled from board member to board member. I even engaged the wives in conversation. Yes, this girl worked the corporate scene, especially when it came to Derrick's career.

I had managed to get through packing up his office with little to no tears. I had collected the pictures of him and I, the trinkets, the awards, and plaques. I took one last look around the corner office. The drawers to the desk were emptied. All his files filled one of the two boxes I had to carry. Derrick's corner office was now bare. Absent of his presence. Void of all his late nights, business conversations, and meetings. It would soon be repainted and ready for a new member of his company to occupy. It represents just another nail I had to hammer down.

I opened the double doors and notified the receptionist that I was done. Margaret was always so nice to me. She was an older woman and wore her years of experience on her face. She reminded me of someone who might have attended secretarial school for girls in the 50's. A woman that clearly wanted a career and independence from the security of a man. After all these years, it had never dawned on me to find out if Margaret had ever gotten married. If she had any of the pain and heartache, I was experiencing, or if we had more in common than being women and this company because we both have always worked to put our best face forward for.

As always, Margaret was on it. There were two men sent to carry boxes out to my car. Margaret hugged me and gave me the warmest smile. I would miss her and her motherly ways.

I walked out of the executive suites into the stares of onlookers. Employees who either worked for Derrick, his peers, or those who coveted the now vacant office and position his absence now left available. I held my head high and suppressed the tears that awaited me for the long ride home. It was the last time I had to work the room for Derrick. The last time I would have to put on a pretty tight face that masked the pain and confusion I had been victim to for years. It was my final goodbye to the doting wife. The ride or die chic that had Derricks back. The subsequential black girl with the magic that had manage to marry a brother of a higher caliber. It was over. The secret was out and now I was left to manage through the pain alone and with the eyes of the world asking how.

The Past

It was the end of my first full year at WMU. It was my last final exam for the semester. I was walking out of the Gilmore Theatre Complex. I had performed my final piece for my grade in Theatre Arts. I had become obsessed with the playwright August Wilson. Mr. Wilson's ability to tell the plight of the Afro-American struggle in early America had made me a fan. It was his play Joe Turner Come and Gone that instantly became one of my all-time favorites. I chose a scene from that play to act with a few of my classmates. I had laid it all on the stage. I poured my emotions out and let the character speak through me. There wasn't a dry eye in the room. I had walked off the stage knowing that I had given my all and was definitely on to something.

I breathed in the warm spring day as I walked back toward my dorm. I could hear someone calling my name from behind me. I knew that it wasn't D'Markus, but it did sound familiar. I turned, trying to figure out who it might be. There he stood. The stranger from many months ago. He flashed a smile, and those dimples reminded me of his generous gesture.

"Tracy!" He said, smiling.

I smiled back as he took my hand by surprise. "Tracy, I've been searching all over for you. You are one of the hardest women to track down." He continued.

I was held in a trance by his dimples, those perfect teeth and his smile.

"Tracy?" He questioned.

"I'm sorry," I apologized as I snapped out of the trance. "Yes" I replied.

"I said you're one of the hardest women to track down. I've been looking for you" the mysterious stranger stated.

"Looking for me, for what?" I questioned.

It must have been my facial expression that gave away my uncomfortableness surrounding his statement.

"Not like that silly. I just wanted to make sure you were okay. Besides, what kind of gentleman would I be if I didn't want to make sure that the prettiest girl on campus was okay." He confirmed as he moved closer to me.

I blushed. "Are you referring to that night? Oh Yeah, I'm good. But thank you." I concluded as I started to walk away.

He ran after me. "Hold up Tracy. Can we talk for a minute? At least let me introduce myself" he uttered slightly out of breath.

"I'm sorry. I just finished my last exam. I still have some packing to do before I head back home." I commented.

"Home, where's home?" He asked

"Buffalo, New York" I answered.

"Ruff Buff, I'm from Brooklyn. We are practically neighbors. Oh, and by the way, I'm Derrick, Derrick Montgomery" he stated with the confidence of a politician.

I stopped walking so that Derrick could catch his breath. "Look, nice to meet you, Derrick. And I think it's cool that we both rep New York, but I really have to get.."

"Look Tracy, all I'm asking for is a few minutes of your time. Can I just take you to get something to eat? I know you hungry, you just finished your last exam, you probably didn't eat beforehand, so let me treat you. And if after you had eaten, then if you gotta go, you can go. I promise." Derrick said with a smile on his face as he crossed his heart and held up his right hand as if to swear an oath.

I paused for a while as I looked into his eyes and he flashed those dimples. "Okay" I responded.

"Girl, you need to say that like you about to have some fun" Derrick jokingly said as he grabbed my hand and danced the hungry dance.

"Fine, Ok! And then I seriously need to go finish packing" I countered by smiling back at him. He led the way and I followed at his side. Little did I know, this would be the start of the end and a complicated journey of love.

The Present

It was an exceedingly small gathering. Derrick had left specific notes for his final funeral arrangements. Even though we had discussed this many times prior to this date, I never thought that I would carry out his plan. Derrick requested that he be cremated. Nothing fancy, just a few spoken words, attended by only closest friends and family. It was supposed to be a private affair. It was the last promise I needed to keep. Even in death, he had managed to manipulate me into doing all he had requested of me—covering up his secret from the world. I didn't know if I should cry, laugh, or scream. Oddly, there was a steeling calm that swept over me. I was numb, and for once, content. Nothing to worry about. Nothing to try to cover up, no one to worry about, no situation or problem to solve. I just sat there and enjoyed the peace that fell over me.

Family and friends gathered at our home for the repass. I had hired a catering company to cook for those paying their respects. Even in this day of Covid-19 and masks, I was still able to see through the bullshit. I could hear the muttered murmurs of his family. Wondering how much money he left me, how would I afford the lifestyle he provided me with—wondering if there was a final will and whether they were entitled to anything. I was wondering how long it would be before the vultures circled.

The few close friends walked about admiring the home that Derrick and I built. The picturesque estate was reserved for the affluent, and here Derrick and I were, two common black folks that had managed to do everything right, despite the inner-city upbringing, living the white American dream. They looked over the furnishings, our pictures outlining the exotic ventures across the globe and the many accomplishments that lined our walls. I couldn't help but notice the pity in their eyes. One could mistake it for empathy, but I was smarter. These were Derrick's friends, not mines. Even after years of marriage, one would think that I had acquired a social circle all my own. That I had a group of friends to surround me and lay hands on me to comfort me in my time of need. And that they would pray over me and nurse my mental and emotional self-back to life. But I was alone. Between my career and Derrick's needs, I was left with little time to have a life outside of this house. I hadn't noticed how much I needed that support until now. Now that I was looking in the faces of people, knowing that their only connection to me, now sat in the urn on the fireplace.

I thanked everyone for coming. Each one of them echoing some pathetic words of condolence, quoting scriptures, and caring proverbs. Offering cliché's like, call me, and I'm here for you. Where were you when Derrick had his episodes? Where were you when I had to walk him off the ledge? Where were you when there were fights about taking his medication? Keep that shit. I'll be just fine. Just like I was when it was me and him. Just like I had been so many nights when I cried in silence because I couldn't call you. They had never been here for me before, so why would today be any different? Why should it matter now? You all looked to him as some sort of savior, hope, or leader figure. Who was I to taint that image of him? Who was I to lay my burden on you? How dare I ask you to carry the baggage that I have toiled with for so many years? No, I could not and would not give you the satisfaction of holding that over me. I just shook my head and whispered, "thank you for coming, I appreciate your coming. Derrick would have loved knowing you were here for me." I lied.

His mother stayed on a few weeks with me. Derrick was her only child. Her husband had died years earlier from a heart attack. Derrick was the spitting image of his father, and he was awfully close to his mother. Me, I had loved them both, but at a distance. They had both made it clear that Derrick was their son, and I was only his wife. I remember at the onset of Derrick's mental illness surfacing, I had asked questions, and his parents took offense. His father told me to be a better wife and maybe his son would act better. His mother told me to pray for him. I wanted answers as to why the man I had married had suddenly become a stranger in my house. Why his erratic mood swings replaced date nights, and how do I cope with his unpredictable roller coaster rides. I wanted off, but they kept pushing me into the line of fire. Yes, the mother of the monster was here with me, and I wanted to offer comfort to her, but my hardened heart forced her to mourn alone.

Ms. Rebecca Lorraine LeBeouf Montgomery was a social elite. As her family's matriarch and the heiress to her family's estate, impressions and status were everything. I know this because she told me as much. When Derrick first introduced me to her, I saw the disgusted look on her face. See, Rebecca had married what she referred to as a commoner. Someone outside of her tribe, or shall I say pedigree. Derrick's father was a blue-collar guy. He had worked his way up the manufacturing chain. In marrying Allen Montgomery, Rebecca lost her inheritance at least until the first-born child graduated college. Until then, she lived like a commoner. Derrick grew up in a brownstone in Brooklyn. It was a beautiful home with ornate wood details throughout. I could tell from the furniture selections that Rebecca had exquisite taste.

I think I slowly won Rebecca over. During my many visits to spend time with Derrick. Rebecca began to see that we had more in common than we both initially thought. My debutant teachings began to pay off. I respected the house by sleeping in a separate room when visiting. After all, Derrick and I weren't married. I assisted around the house and even cooked dinner a few times. I accompanied her on her outings. I gave fashion advice when asked and even managed to make her smile. Slowly, she began to see that I had the best interest for him, the same way she had. And that would become our bond. Yes, Derrick was the glue that held us together. He would also be the reason we fell apart.

I was up earlier than normal. I couldn't sleep. It was almost time for my 3:30 alarm to go off, signaling time for me to head to the local gym. I had made my way down to the kitchen, turned on the light, and there in the dark sat Rebecca at the kitchen nook.

The sadness in her eyes spoke all the words she could not express. My turning on the light startled her.

"Good Morning Rebecca. I didn't mean to startle you. What are you doing up?" I asked, already knowing the answer.

She motioned to her cup of coffee and smiled.

"May I join you for a few minutes?" I asked politely.

She nodded as if to say yes. Rebecca was never one to keep silent for long. I'm sure under the circumstances, silence may have been the healing she needed right now. I watched as she stared out the window into the backyard. You could hear the early morning callings of the birds as they sang in anticipation of the sun. Her face looked tired and old. Like she had held onto life and love but was left with nothing but regret and sorrow. I had almost finished my morning shake and was about to leave out for a much-needed workout when she finally spoke the evil that lay silent within her.

"You Killed him. You killed my son, didn't you?" she crossed her eyes and stared at me. I stood in silence as she continued. "My Derrick is dead because of you, because of you!" she screamed out in pain.

I began to walk away. There was no way I was going to tolerate this bullshit at 3:54 in the morning.

"Don't you walk away from me when I'm talking to you" she cried.

"You could have saved him; you could have stopped him. Instead, you chose to let him die" she continued.

I had managed to make my way back over to her. Raising my hand in the air, I quickly brought it down and connected with her face. I had slapped Rebecca into reality. She was stunned at my calming gesture.

"I did everything I could for your son. I cooked, cleaned, endured his foolishness, counted his pills, went looking for him in the middle of the night when he had an episode. I did everything short of following him around 24/7 to make sure he didn't harm himself. So, fuck you Rebecca. Where were you when I asked about your family's medical records? Oh, let me recall, that's right, I need to pray about it, or what was it your husband said me, that I need to be a better wife. I had been the best damn wife I could have been, and it still didn't make a difference. He killed himself. He killed our relationship the moment he refused to take his pills. He was dead the moment he stopped going to therapy. You know what? I died too. I died every time he didn't come home. Every time he mixed alcohol with his medicine. I died every time he went on an emotional rollercoaster and didn't want to get off. I cried, I prayed, I hid his dirty little secrets to keep his image, the image of your son in tack. I played doting wife so that he could keep a job, so that everyone could think that Derrick was this great loving man. But the truth is your son was in pain. The pain I couldn't even imagine. Pain so great that the only way he could be at peace was to kill himself. That is not my fault. It's no one's fault. If you want to blame anyone, blame yourself for not disclosing the fact that your family has a history of mental illness. That you also struggle with it. Oh yes, I've seen the medicine bottles. Prescription names that I know all too well. If anyone killed him, it was you. You and your perfect world, perfect son. He killed himself to get away from all of it, including you." I wailed as the tears rolled down my face.

I walked away, knowing that the words I spoke stung. That the pain I felt was now hers to endure. I could not hold back. She needed to sit there in that house of pain with the images I held on to. The many nights of tantrums, fits of anger, and bouts of pain that I nursed her son out of. She needed to see him for who he was, and not the image she created in her mind. I was done covering up Derrick's secret life. The gym awaited and the first thing I was going to do was hit that punching bag before I hit someone in its place.

The Past

All it took was an impromptu meal with great conversation, and when I was done eating, I knew that Derrick was someone I could see me spending the rest of my life with. He was everything D'Markus wasn't, but I had wished he were. I knew I didn't want the day to end. He followed me back to my dorm and helped me pack. We continued talking. We discussed everything and anything. It felt so natural, honest, and real. We exchanged phone numbers and promised to keep in touch over the summer.

What I didn't expect to happen was Derrick coming to visit me back home in Buffalo. Derrick had me pick him up from the airport. He had rented a hotel room and was here for the week. I had managed to change my shift at Quality Markets to the early mornings. I would go to work in the deli at the store on Kenmore and Delaware from 5:30 am and be done by 1:30 pm. When my shift ended, Derrick had managed to find his way to the supermarket. He would pick me up and drop me off home in the rental car he booked. We would spend every moment together. On the first visit, it was all about us getting to know each other. By his fourth visit, I was spending the night with him and loving every moment. He had met my friends and family. They totally adored him.

I was quickly falling in love with him., and he made it easy. He was a gentleman. He motivated me to be my best. He made me feel secure and safe. Something that I had never had with D'Markus. Yeah, he offered protection, but with Derrick, my heart felt safe. Like I could always count on him. That he would never let me down. I was falling for him badly and I didn't want it to stop.

It was my turn to make the trip to Brooklyn. Derrick had informed me that his parents were excited to meet me. Derrick had only brought only one girl home. Shawna James. He told me that his mother absolutely hated her. No mother likes the new woman in her son's life. I'm sure there wasn't anything wrong with Shawna, nothing besides, she chose the wrong guy to love because mothers of sons can be controlling. I had experienced that with D'Markus's mom. I anticipated staying in a hotel, but Derrick insisted that I stay at his parents' home.

I arrived at LaGuardia Airport on time. Then made my way to the baggage claim. A short stocky guy was holding a sign with my name on it. He was dressed in an ill-fitting black suit. I walked up to him and told him who I was. He smiled, grabbed my bags, and welcomed me to New York. I followed closely behind him as we exited the bustling terminal. He opened the back door on the passenger side of the town car. I hurried myself in as if my debutante training were on full display. Paulie introduced himself to me as we made the journey to my destination. He pointed out all the typical sights of interest. It was great being in the city. The hustle and bustle of the big apple was exciting. It took my mind off of the fact that I was meeting his parents. And from everything that Derrick told me, I knew I would like them too.

I was wearing a cute summer dress. It was mint green with white flowers. I wore a pair of nude, 3-inch peep-toe pumps that I had put on in the car. My white Cardigan draped over my Dooney tan leather duck purse. My hair was bone straight and hung just below my shoulders. I contemplated adding extensions, but Derrick loved me natural. My face was complemented by a light covering of make-up and my favorite lip gloss from MAC dressed my lips. I was ready. though not too much, but a respectable presentation for meeting Derrick's parents.

After spending time in traffic, hearing Paulie cuss a few times, and horns blaring, we had pulled up in front of a beautiful Brownstone. The street was lined with small cherry blossom trees. There were families out and about enjoying the day. I loved the vibe that Brooklyn was offering me. It gave way to understanding many of the traits that I loved about Derrick. I could tell that this was his hood, even with all the formalities that came with his upbringing. There was still a little street in Derrick, and it was nice to see where that came from.

Derrick met me at the front door. His mother and father followed close behind. They greeted me with hugs, as Derrick grabbed my bags and thanked Paulie for delivering me safe and sound. I entered their home. It was beautiful. I've always loved the detailing on older homes. The wood built-ins and the fireplace were original accents to the home. The rich mahogany echoed throughout the house. From the staircase, the cabinets and Derrick's dad's office. The wood floors added to the masculine character of the home. Mrs. Montgomery invited me to make myself comfortable. I sat in the living room while

Derrick placed my bags in my room. His dad carried a tray of iced tea into the living room while his mother carried the tray of petit fours.

Thank goodness for all the etiquette classes and debutant grooming. I did everything that Ms. Ella had instructed. My legs were crossed at my ankles, and my napkin was perfectly placed on my lap. I only took two of the bite size treats from the floral printed china plate. I took small bites as we engaged in small talk. They asked about my flight and the ride over. I gave them my mother's information for emergency purposes. Mrs. Montgomery had laid out her plans for the two of us to get acquainted. Mr. Montgomery just shook his head, laughing. Derrick sat there just staring at me. His smiles made the questions and awkwardness fade away.

By the third day, I had been to Manhattan and Times Square. I had visited the Country Club and had lunch with Mrs. Montgomery and her friends. We went shopping and sightseeing while Derrick was at his internship. It was fun, but every day at 6 pm, I awaited his arrival. It was like a wife waiting for her husband. It was the role I felt I was born to play. After all, Derrick made it easy. He was so attentive and caring. We would eat dinner and I got to hear all about his day. We all had questions. His father, a blue-collar worker was proud that his son would be a college graduate and could someday make partner at a firm. His mother basked in the joys of having her only child home for the summer and would welcome any conversation they were having. I listened. I listened to the excitement that resonated with every story Derrick told about his day. I gave him suggestions on how he should respond or move the next time a situation similar to the one he explained. I gave him insight on what his employer might be looking for. Instructed him to take the initiative and also encouraged him to stand out from the other interns. His father smiled at me when I chimed in.

"Son, you need to listen to Tracy. She's on to something." He would say.

Rebecca would just smile and nod in agreeance with me. I could tell she was watching me, and the way Derrick and I interacted. I was excited for Derrick. We all were. He was entering his last year of college and landing a job of his dreams was so close to the internship he had this summer. It was important that I show my support. His parents needed to see that I was sincere in my feelings for their son.

After dinner, Derrick would show me around his neighborhood. Every day, I had an opportunity to see a little bit more about Derrick. To understand what makes him who he is. I enjoyed our long walks and deep talks. And before I knew it, the week was over, and it was time for me to go back home. I knew that if we kept this up, it would become harder to leave and easier to stay. This summer was full of surprises, and I could not wait for the fall semester to begin. This way, I could see Derrick every day without the back and forth, distance and time between us.

The Present

———————— ❧ ————————

It had been days since Ms. Rebecca had graced me with her presence. Her flight back to Brooklyn was leaving first thing in the morning. Not that I was counting the minutes, but I certainly needed time to myself. I had offered her an opportunity to go through Derrick's things. I figured as his mom, there might be a few mementos she would like to hold on to. I made sure she had plenty of obituaries to share with her family and friends. I even wrapped up a few framed pictures of him; I wanted her to have.

My motives had become selfish. I knew good and well, Rebecca should stay right where she was, in this big ole' empty house with me. Lord knows I did not need her falling into a deep depression and harming herself. I just felt like she needed some time. That I needed time to breathe too. I'm sure that once we both have had an opportunity to grieve in our own time, space and place, we would be able to communicate and work through Derrick's passing together.

We were up bright and early like it was Christmas morning. Ms. Rebecca was packed, polished and primmed. She sat at the kitchen nook with a smug look on her face. She sat with her back to me. I made us sunny side up eggs, bagels with her standard two slices of turkey bacon and avocado slices. We ate in silence. We occasionally glanced in each other's direction, but no words or pleasantries. I cleaned up the kitchen, packed my stuff into the car and off we headed to the airport. God forbid I send her off in a car service. I would never hear the end of it. So, I did the noble thing and made sure that she was taken care of. Derrick would have wanted it this way.

We were early at the airport. I opted for valet service and paid for baggage assistance. I walked with Ms. Rebecca at her side. I took stride for stride as I allowed her to process the events of the past few weeks. With each step, I could feel the resistance. Her breathing became heavier. Her pace slowed, and the tears she held back began to stream down her face and scarred the perfectly placed makeup she contoured to hide her age spots. I caught her in my arms as she leaned off to the left. I caught her as she trusted me to anchor her lifeless body. It had been too much for her to burden. A load that she could no longer carry. Her heart had been broken, and there were no words to mend it. I sat there with her in my arms like a child, holding her as she cried for her son. As she owned every wrong that she had done to protect him and everything right she had done to save him. Derrick was gone, and Ms. Rebecca had eaten my words and digested her part in the criminalization of her son's mental illness. It was the medicine she had refused to take, and I gave it to her a dosage too high to manifest. Yet here we were in the middle of the airport, me wishing my words tasted sweeter and her wishing her words had meaning.

The Past

The semester was underway. It was the beginning of my junior year. Derrick and I had moved in together at the end of last year. It just made sense, especially since he was now working and no longer a student. At least not right now. He had plans to attend Graduate School next semester. We lived in an apartment complex off of KL Ave. It was tucked away and semi secluded. It was a modest 2-bedroom, 1.5 bath apartment. It was a far cry from the dorms and yet nothing like the brownstone or home I grew up in. The only thing that mattered was Derrick and I was there together.

I would attend classes during the day while Derrick was at work. In his short tenure at the CPA Firm, Derrick had made junior partner. It was an exciting time. We were both learning our way and exploring our life together. I had come to know that Derrick snored and preferred peach marmalade over Grape Jelly. He liked the crust cut off of this bread when having sandwiches. He loved cookies and cream ice cream and slept on the right side of the bed. I immersed myself into everything about Derrick, and I loved it.

I made sure dinner was ready by the time Derrick arrived home. I would study while he completed any work he brought home. Weekends were made for us. No school or work unless when absolutely necessary. Saturday's were deeded lazy Saturdays, reserved for movies, date night, and hanging with friends. Sundays, we would have dinner, clean, and prepare for the week ahead. It was family life without the ring and signed document. Which I knew would soon be happening.

Derrick worked really hard most weeknights. The pressure he was under, I wasn't sure if it was self-induced or if it was truly the demand of the job. Derrick would always get so low and bothered by what appeared to be the smallest issue. Everything needed to be perfect, even when it wasn't. Some nights he was just the happiest person to be around. He would joke with me and even took breaks for sex. He would listen to me rehearse my lines and even read over my papers for class. He seemed at peace. Then there were other times that he would get so upset, frustrated and mad. It was like a rollercoaster ride at times. I never knew who I was getting from day to day. Thank goodness for the gym and yoga. That seemed to keep him calm most days. But when the shit hit the fan, and the workload increased, beware of the eye of the storm that was Derrick.

I recall coming home after hanging out with some friends. I found Derrick in the corner of our bedroom, balled up in a fetal position crying uncontrollably. I ran to his side and held him. I had never seen him like this before. It scared me because I didn't know what was wrong. I was finally able to get him in the shower and then into bed. He slept within minutes. The next morning, he woke up a new person with no real memory of the night before. I just thought he was playing it off or that he did not wish to talk about it. I respected his privacy enough to back off when he told me he was ok. I didn't believe him and brushed it off as having to do with being the boy genius at work and trying to complete his master's degree.

All I knew was the pressure he was under was starting to take a toll on him, and there was nothing I could do to help. I just made sure that the things I could control in our little apartment I did. At least I could be his peace in a time of stress.

The Present

A few weeks had passed since Derrick died. I had managed to work every day. I came home, ate dinner, watched my favorite shows, paid bills and thumbed through social media. It was a routine I was accustomed to, but with the exception that Derrick's laughter was vacant from the house. I repeated my routine nightly out of habit and a reluctance to face what has happened. Loneliness started to set in, and soon the darkness took over.

I couldn't get out of bed. My body hurt and I found it difficult to breathe. My heart would pound, and my laughter slowly turned to tears. There were days that I could not even bother to bathe myself or comb my hair. I ached all over. And unlike a cold or flu, no medicine was able to dull the pain. It had me paralyzed. I watch video after video of my life with Derrick. I drowned in the laughter and wanted so much to hear his voice. I wanted to talk with him. I wanted him to run his hands through my hair. Hold me tight in his arms and kiss the back of my neck while we slept. I missed him. I missed my friend and needed him to know that it would have gotten better if he had just held on a little longer. That he could have gotten the help he needed, that he did not have to do this. But instead, I just watch the happy times of our marriage like a sitcom. My tears and cries played like the broken album with a scratch embedded in it.

I called my human resource department and took a few days off work. The days turned into weeks, and before I knew it, I was out on FMLA. I had never experienced depression like this before. Yes, I would occasionally become depressed. Smile through the trauma of dealing with Derrick's episodes. But to be physically impaired by it, never. I had managed to accept my human resource department's request to seek the counseling of a trained psychologist. It was one of the only times that I made myself presentable. It was a virtual appointment through ZOOM, which seemed to be the new normal these days. With Covid-19 restrictions still in place, in person doctor visits were not being conducted at this time. In person visits were reserved for the severely ill. I know I witnessed the hospital turning away family members when I sat in my car, waiting for news on Derrick. It was something that I had never witnessed before, especially for such a public place for care.

Dr. Mary was a gentle soul. The older gray-haired woman's kind voice always greeted me with a smile. Her signature red lipstick stained her overly wrinkled lips while the rouge blush counterbalanced the brightness against her pale aged face.

"Hello Tracy, how are you today?" That's how Dr. Mary would always start our sessions.

And I would always lie, "I'm doing okay," I would reply.

"Good. Let's start our session," she would continue.

After we exchanged small talk and recapped the previous session, we were well under way. I tried to remain focused. At times, my mind would drift to times where I had encouraged Derrick to seek out counseling, and then to the times that he actually did talk with a professional, and then to times where it seemed he had given up completely. I attempted to be transparent with Dr. Mary, but I had been lying for so long, and I was afraid to confront my own demons.

Today's topic was addressing why I was so angry. I had mentioned during a previous conversation that I was angry all the time. And here, it resurfaced to bite me in the ass. I could only imagine all the notes that Dr. Mary had taken on me. I had never considered myself a nut case, but I'm sure the few screws I had were as lose as or missing by now after the year I was having. I felt like I was living someone else's life. And by the look of it, I was not playing the role very well.

I began to tell Dr. Mary about my anger. How I tried for years to get Derrick the help he needed, and for years he resisted me. He even hated me at times. That I was angry about him leaving me the way he did even though I should have left him years ago. How I felt trapped in a marriage I could not win. That I was pissed that his parents knew there was a possibility that Derrick could be suffering from mental illness, but because they wanted him to be their perfect child, they never had him tested. And how, even when they found out, they turned a blind eye. I was frustrated over the lies that I had told to cover up for Derrick's behavior. How I had excused him and never held him accountable for anything. And how for years I accepted it. I just sat there and allowed myself to be emotionally and mentally manipulated, all so that Derick and I could save face. I was angry because right now, at this moment, I couldn't even express this to him. After all, he isn't here anymore. That I never had an opportunity to tell him how I felt. How unhappy I had been. How alone I was in our marriage and how much I hated him for calling after me that day in the campus courtyard. If only I had said no to lunch with him. If only I had walked away. If only I hadn't fallen in love with him, maybe, just maybe, I could have saved my heart.

There I said it. I was angry. I was pissed off. I was upset. I was mad. I was alone. I was confused. I was heartbroken. I was relieved.

The Past

It was graduation day! I was so excited. I thought this day would never arrive. I was graduating Western Michigan University with a degree in Business Management and a Minor in Theatre Arts. Right by my side was Derrick, graduating with his Accounting MBA. And just when I thought the day couldn't get any better, I stepped off the stage and was greeted by Derrick, his mom, dad, my mom, stepfather, my sorority sisters and a host of friends. It was also the night Derrick got down on one knee in front of everyone and spoke the most eloquent words, and had asked me to marry him. I said yes.

I was now starting my new job as the Head of Business Sales and Market for a local social media firm. I wouldn't call it my dream job, but it was close. It was going to give me the background and experience I would need to one day be a successful entrepreneur in the cyberworld. I was also heavily involved with the planning of the wedding. Between my mom and Derrick's mother were calls and texts of suggestions, recommendations and pictures. I was so exhausted. Derrick was working hard, and most nights, we barely had time to speak, but we held true to our week rituals. Saturdays were reserved for lazy days and offered us a chance to reconnect and no work was allowed. Sundays, we attended church per his mother's request. We then cleaned the house and rested.

It was two months before the September wedding date. It was Friday night, and Derrick had promised to come straight home. We had to work on the seating chart for the reception. Five o'clock came and went. Seven, eight, ten and eleven o'clock passed me by. I had tried calling him several times, but his phone went straight to voice mail. I was starting to worry. I sat there trying to stay positive, but all I could think about was him lying injured somewhere or, worse dead. I was losing my mind. Where was he? I prayed he was ok.

I woke to a knock on the door. The constant pounding reminded me of life in the inner city. We called it the police knock. It was relentless and loud. I jumped up and quickly turned on the lights and peeked out the window. There was a police car in the driveway. My heart sank. I held back the tears as I ran toward the door. When I opened it, there stood Derrick, accompanied by a police officer. He was missing his shoes, and the dress shirt that matched his suit was missing. He looked disoriented and confused. He looked at me like a sad puppy that had desecrated the carpet when its owner was not looking. He looked frightened, standing there in front of me. I gasped. I hugged him and welcomed him home. I instructed the police to come in so that we could talk.

Derrick had made his way upstairs while I sat with the police officers, who began to spin a tale, I would not have believed if they had not told me themselves. I was at a loss for words. I didn't know what to say. They had asked if he was on any medication, if he had a history of mental illness, and if he had ever done anything like this before. My heart and mind were still attempting to process the events that had been shared with me. I answered with uncertainty. I hadn't known Derrick to be on any medication other than his One-A-Day vitamins and an occasional Excedrin for his migraines. I shook my head no and continued to listen to their muttered words. My zombie state left me confused and with more questions than answers.

"Wait, where is his car? Where did you say this happen again? I am sorry this is all too much for me to... "I uttered.

"Mrs. Montgomery, we can tell this is a lot to hear right now. Here is my card. Call me if you have any questions. Please get your husband some help. It sounds like you two may have a lot to discuss," the officer said.

I walked them to the door. I thank them for bringing Derrick home. Then I closed the door behind them and watched the tears flow from my eyes in the foyer mirror.

A few days had passed since the incident. I watched Derrick walk around as if nothing had happened. I was still trying to make sense of everything the police officer had disclosed to me. I didn't know if I should hit him, cry, or just leave.

I wished that I had ran. I was tired of being upset. I was tired of the silent treatment that I was giving him. I had not cooked in days and was too mentally drained to fight. Derrick just went about his days as if nothing had changed. Like nothing had happened. And according to the officer, more than enough took place that Friday night. With less than two months before I was to say I do, doubt had reared its ugly head, and I had concerns about the man I had chosen to be my husband.

The Present

⁓

"Tracy Montgomery, David will see you now" the slender receptionist called out.

I stood up and followed her through the double glass doors and into the spacious glass floor to ceiling lined office. I had never been to this attorney's office. I was surprised by the letter requesting a meeting to discuss Derrick's affairs. We had already had the will reading. I was unsure why my attendance was requested, but I obliged and was eager to find out what this was all about. I didn't think that there were any secrets between Derrick and I, then again, I also didn't think that Derrick would ever take his own life.

David Vanderwater was a statuesque figure. He stood about "6'2", with baby blond hair and intense green eyes. He had a natural tan glow that made his skin look like those that frequent the French Riviera. His suit was well tailored, and his smile welcomed me as I entered his office.

"Please be seated" David gestured, pointing to the leather chairs adjacent to his desk. "I know this may seem a little strange, me requesting that we meet in person, especially with the pandemic in full force." He stated while placing his mask over his face.

"Yes, I was quite surprised by your letter, and I was curious to find out what it is that you need me for. So please tell me what I can do for you?" I questioned.

David pulled out a file folder the size of a book. He began to tell a story that I could not believe. It reminded me of the events that transpired years earlier. The night that Derrick was accompanied home by the police. The night I should have ran. I could feel my heart breaking yet again. Just when I thought that Derrick's reach and hold on me had ended, even in death he had managed to place me in situations that I had little control over or made me the evil bitch most people perceived me to be.

He handed me a package of information. His instructions were simple. I was only to know about the contents in the envelope in the event something had happened to Derrick, and there was no one else to assist. And unfortunately, according to David, this burden had fallen on me, just like so many burdens I had carried for Derrick. I was now left to figure out his sins that plagued his existence and now haunted me in mine. I now had a greater issue to resolve. Would I be the understanding wife and hide behind my ignorance, or would I be the bitch everyone assumed I was? I wish I knew which role I was best suited for. Damn you Derrick, Damn you.

I left the office and hurried to my car. I sat there in silence. It was too late to be angry. He would never know, nor could he care how upset I was. I attempted to use the breathing exercises Dr. Mary had suggested I did when feeling overwhelmed, but that shit was not working right now. I felt the heat from the information covering me. I felt lightheaded, nauseous and week. Something wasn't right. My head began to spin and before I knew it, everything went dark.

The Past

I was finally Mrs. Derrick Allen Montgomery! I was on my way to the Secretary of State office to complete my name change on my driver's license. This would make everything official. I was there first thing in the morning, just as the doors to the building were being opened. I was the third person in line and before I could even take a seat, my number was called, the picture had been taken, and my temporary paper license had been issued. I looked down and remembered thinking just how lucky I was.

The next stop, was for my doctor's appointment. I hadn't been feeling well for a few days. Derrick suggested that I see my doctor being that we were out of the country for our honeymoon. He wanted to rule out any foreign contagions and to make sure it wasn't too serious. I agreed. I arrived right on time. I had checked in and before long, the lively nurse called me back to the office for my checkup. The nurse took my vitals, gave me the standard hospital robe to put on, then she left the room. I took my clothing off and draped it over the patient's chair. I sat down on the exam table and waited for the knock on the door.

Dr. Houser entered the room within five minutes of me waiting and starting a solitaire game on my phone. He asked what had brought me in today. I told him about my honeymoon to Mexico and that upon my return from my trip, I started feeling ill. He congratulated me on my recent nuptials as he began to place the stethoscope on my chest and asked me to breath in and out. He listened to my lungs and checked my glands. He then asked an interesting question: Could I be pregnant? I had never thought that this could have been the issue. Sure, I was on birth control, but I could not recall taking my pills faithfully over the past few weeks. With the stress of the wedding and the pressing issue with Derrick, I could have forgotten to take my pills a few times.

With the vague answer that I gave Dr. Houser, he suggested that we do a test. I was handed a sterilized urine capture cup and instructions on how to wipe myself for a clean sample. I followed the directions and before long was handing the wrapped container to the nurse for analysis. I headed back to my exam room and waited. A million thoughts rushed through my mind. Could I be? Were we ready? What kind of mother would I be? What about Derrick? What about my career? I had never been so relieved to hear the knock on the door as Dr. Houser entered the room. I thought for sure his words would lead to a prescription for some kind of virus that could be cured. But he spoke the words that I did not expect to hear. "Tracy, congratulations, your pregnant!" Dr. Houser said in an exciting tone.

I was stunned. I was going to be a mom. I had just become someone's wife and now, we were already planning on adding to our family. How would Derrick take the news? I was not sure, but he was soon going to find out. Dr. Houser had scheduled an immediate ultrasound so that we could confirm what he had suspected. With the stress of the wedding, honeymoon, and work, I might be further along than he suspected. I got dressed and made my way over to the ultrasound testing suite. I waited for about ten minutes before being escorted back to the ultrasound room. The ultrasound technician was young but assured me that she would be able to assist me. She took the time to explain to me the process. She went on to tell me that Dr. Houser ordered a vaginal view as well as a standard view of my abdomen. She gave me the cloth gown to put on. I was to remove all clothing from the waist down. She gave me a sheet to drape over my lower body. I waited with anticipation for her return.

She returned, and the testing was underway. The jelly was warmed before the technician applied it to my stomach area. She pressed down and moved the wand across my abdomen. And just like that, on the screen, in black and white, was the image I had not known but was delighted to see—a baby. I was going to be a mom! The tears flowed down my cheeks. There was a rush of emotions that fell over me. I watched as the wand glided over my stomach and she captured frame after frame of the new bundle of joy that lay inside me. After we were done with that, we completed the vaginal ultrasound. The technician took additional pictures for Dr. Houser. When we were done, I wiped my body clean of the jelly, got dressed and waited. When the technician confirmed that her supervisor approved the pictures, I was given a few pictures to take with me. I smiled brightly.

I stared at the images. My heart was full, and I could not wait to share them with my husband. I did not even know that I could feel this way. I was sure that Derrick would be just as excited at hearing the news.

The Present

Therapy day could not have come at a better time. There was so much on my mind. This fucker, this asshole, Derrick. I could not believe him. He'd better be happy that he was dead because I would have loaded my 9mm gun and killed him myself. I felt like I was going to explode. I felt like everything I had loved in my marriage, every promise, all the years amounted to nothing but wasted history, heartache, and pain. What a waste. "What a fucking waste of my entire life!" I cried out loud as the tears became streams of regret, and my face soaked in the thunder of pain.

Dr. Mary knew right away that something was wrong. Her kind words allowed me to release a cancer that had manifested itself inside me for the past 2 days. It was time to release and let go. To finally confront my issues. To heal myself. To let Derrick go and find a way to move past the pain. So today, I decided just to let it flow. To let the truth out once and for all. I had to, or it was going to destroy me. So, I did just that. I started with the night that changed our marriage.

"Derrick was escorted home by the police. He had been picked up for disorderly conduct. They found him with a woman. She claimed that they had just met at the bar. They had a few drinks. Things got a little hot and heavy, so they went across the street to a hotel. Apparently, they had sex, according to the police officer, and then things got out of control. According to the woman, Derrick started rambling and speaking almost in another language, which is funny because he doesn't speak any other languages. The officer went on to say that Derrick's behavior took a sharp turn. He opened the window to the hotel room. The room was on the fourth floor. The woman tried to get Derrick to calm down and move away from the open window, but he became enraged. She immediately called the front desk for help and they called 911. By the time we arrived, Derrick was hanging out the window, one leg in one leg out. We managed to get him back in the room. By the time we were able to calm him down, the paramedics had arrived, but he had passed out." I paused and allowed myself to be ok, verbalizing for the first time what happened so many years ago.

Dr. Mary sat in silence. She was writing her thoughts and my thoughts down on her note pad. "Tracy, how long have you held that information in?" she asked.

"Since the day I found out. It was the first of many secrets that I kept of Derrick's. I didn't want to believe any of it. It was so out of character for him. And to make things worse, he did not recall any of it. The police said that when he finally came around, he seemed disorientated and confused. All he kept saying was Tracy, where is my wife Tracy. The officer had checked his wallet for Identification. That was how they knew where to bring him. I tried talking to him about what happened, but he honestly did not recall anything past leaving for work and the headache that followed the next day. I wanted so much to believe him. We were getting married in less than two months. Nothing about what the officer told me made any sense. It just wasn't the Derrick I knew." I confessed.

"So, you never had an opportunity to hear his side of the story?" Dr. Mary questioned.

"Dr. Mary, he didn't remember. The look in his eyes told me that he believed everything that he said. He kept asking why I kept questioning him about that night. I just couldn't bring myself to repeat the story the officer shared. So, I just let it go. I kept it to myself. I decided at that moment that I would never speak of it again, and I married him instead. Even though that was the first red flag, but I chose to ignore it." I lamented!

"Why are you sharing this now?" Dr. Mary inquired.

"I'm getting to that." I replied agitatedly. "Fast forward a few months. We had just arrived home from our honeymoon. I wasn't feeling well. Derrick suggested that I go to the doctor and make sure that it was not a tropical virus. I made an appointment. To my surprise, I was pregnant. After about 11 weeks, with all the stress of the wedding, the issue with Derrick, I hadn't noticed the changes in my body. I just chalked it up to being stressed out. But there I was, pregnant, excited and scared. I went home to share the good news with Derrick. But he also had news to share with me." Then I paused.

"What was his news" Dr. Mary quizzed.

"He told me that a woman called him today. She had one of his business cards. That they had met one night at a bar downtown a few months back. She asked if I could meet her to discuss something important. I thought she was a potential client. But at that moment in his story, I knew what was coming next. I recalled every detail that the officer shared with me that night. I sat there in shock, shaking my head. My heart sank to the floor; I started crying. I couldn't hear Derrick's voice, but I had read his lips as the events of that night echoed loud and clear. I had heard it once before, so there was no need for me to hear it again. Derrick fell to his knees in front of me and begged me to understand. He could not recall if any of the events he expressed happened, and that he would never do anything to hurt me. That he didn't want this, that he just didn't understand how something like this could happen. The pain in his eyes. The mix of emotions that came over me. All I could do was slap him in the face." I confessed.

"What happened next?" Dr. Mary asked as she sat up in her chair.

"I tried to push away from him, but he just held me in his arms, trying to reassure me that he didn't do it. That he would never do anything to hurt me, and yet, there I was, pregnant with Derrick's baby, and so was the woman from the night he didn't come home. How could this be happening to me? I was supposed to be in marital bliss, starry eyed and in love. But the day I thought we had proof of that love was the day I found out Derrick had proof of his infidelity. He claimed he could not have done this. But how could I believe him? If it wasn't him, then who was it? And why would anyone lie about him in such a way?" I finished.

The Past

———— ❧ ————

I was numb. I didn't even get a chance to share my news with Derrick. He had gone first and ruined the surprise by disclosing his own little surprise. I slept in the guest bedroom. I hadn't seen him since last night. When I walked out of the locked room, there he was, squatting at the door entrance. He looked like he had been there all night, crying from the look of things. I walked past him. I was emotionally drained. I just did not have the energy to deal with him. I made my way downstairs to the kitchen. I grabbed a glass of water and sat at the kitchen island. Somehow, I just knew that this was not the Saturday I had envisioned after telling my husband that I was carrying his child.

Derrick followed close behind me. He watched me. He was wearing the same clothing from last night, and he was smelling of stale brandy and yesterday's cologne. I could not bear to look at him. I just sat in silence, wondering how this could have happened. Derrick sat across from me. I held back the tears for as long as I could. I was beyond upset; I was furious. Still, all I wanted was for him to hold me and tell me everything would be ok. But I knew different. There was no way that in less than a month of marriage that we could move past this. I wasn't sure I wanted to.

I managed to get myself dressed and combed my hair into a ponytail. I needed to get out of the house. I couldn't stay here another moment. So, I ran. I wasn't sure where I was going, but I knew I wasn't staying either. I thought about going home, but I could hear my mother's voice of eerie disapproval. Her passive aggressive advice always annoyed me to my core. I could not stomach telling her about my newly failed marriage. I thought about going to one of my sorority sisters who lived in Lansing, Michigan, but she was having issues within her marriage. How could I lay my burden on her when I have been a sounding board for her many nights? My advice would be void of meaning and possibly lead her down a path we both could not return from. I was a woman with no place to go. A soul tormented by my own ideas of a fairy tale that now deferred, static and not worth repeating. I had claimed nothing but heartache and the notion that I may have in fact led myself to this path by not listening to my intuition, discrediting my own voice, and turning away from my reasoning just to say I'm Married Now. So, I wandered around town like a lost soul.

I made my way to the airport area. Rode the curved streets, taking Michigan lefts before parking in the lot facing the Days Inn Hotel. There were no more tears: just emptiness and tired eyes. I had driven all over Portage and Kalamazoo. I attempted to go shopping as therapy for my depressed state. There was nothing I could buy that would undo the pain or lack of faith I now had in the institution I willingly engaged in. I did stop to eat dinner. I sat downtown at the Union Bistro and ate in solitude. Then I heard the jazz playing in the background of my cluttered mind. But it was blurred out by the muddled events of the last 24 hours. I wanted to drink myself to slumber but had managed to remember that I was pregnant and cursed to share this blessing with another woman.

I exited the car, then I walked into the hotel and made my way to the service desk. I booked a room, asking if I could leave the reservation open to renew if I decided to stay a few days. I had grabbed my shopping bag from Walgreens and slid into the room I was assigned. I had travel size essentials to make my stay tolerable. I had paid with a credit card that was only in my name. The last thing I wanted was for Derrick to come charging in to sweep me off my feet and flash his deep dimples, and then carry me off into confusion. The sad thing is, I may have let him. Deep down, I really wished he would. I wanted him to be the image of the man I fixed in my mind to be. He was everything I thought I needed and wanted; I don't know what made me think he was any different than those other men in my past. At some point, I concluded that I was destined to be disappointed. I should have placed my value of worth on myself and not on the size of the carat on display on my left hand.

I woke up rested. Despite the anger and other emotions, I felt there was a calm about me. I had slept for almost fifteen hours. I slept past the required check out time, past breakfast and lunch. It was well after 6 pm, and the sun was on its way to setting. The great thing about this time of year was the crisp air and the earth's deep colors that leave a scar on your imagination that you could not ignore. Unlike the fifty missed calls from Derrick, I was always captivated by the sights of fall. I wanted to enjoy the rest of the day while the colors were in view. I took a shower, put on joggers and a long sleeve t-shirt I purchased from JC Penny. The jean jacket and crispy white K-Swiss finished off my outfit. I informed the lady at the front desk that I would indeed be staying at least another night. She smiled as I walked away. Today, I was better than yesterday. I wasn't sure what that meant, but I knew my emotions were no longer leading me. Logic had set in, and I was strategizing my next move.

I made my way out toward the Richland area. I stopped at Gull Meadow Farm to pick up some donuts and cider. It was the end of the apple picking season. They were not as busy as they usually would have been, which was ok with me. I enjoyed looking at the trees that were littered with the colors of autumn. This was something Derrick and I enjoyed every year since being together. Today I realized just how much I enjoyed doing those things with him. His absence was duly noted. I made my way back to the city. I stopped for sushi. I wasn't sure if I could eat certain things, especially now in my condition. But I was craving it, even if it's something horribly, and I was giving in. I would just read up on pregnancy do's and don'ts later. For now, California and Spicy Tuna rolls had won.

Derrick had called yet again, another thirty times. I wasn't ready to speak with him yet. What would I even say? Where would we even begin this conversation? I hadn't even told him about our baby. What could he possibly have to say to me that has not been said? I was not even sure if I was ready to receive his words yet. It was best that we stay right where we were for the moment. So, when his name flashed across the screen yet again, I opted to turn my phone off and made the ride back to the hotel.

The Present

———— ⌇ ————

D r. Mary had suggested that we have multiple sessions this week. After my confessional outcry, she knew I had more that I needed to talk about. Today's session kicked off just like any other conversation. Dr. Mary asked how I was feeling today, and I would respond. The only difference was, I was now honest with my feelings. I guess after you start to lift the restraints, the floodgates open up and you're forced to deal with your shit. It was clearly the reason my eyes were brown.

So, I continued to spill the tea to Dr. Mary. "Derrick and I agreed to work things out. We agreed that he would ask Jessica to have an abortion. He would pay for it, and that would be the end of that. The only children we would be bringing into our family would be the ones I gave birth to. Derrick told me she agreed to have the abortion and I was relieved by her decision. I had hoped we would be able to move past this. I needed to focus on bringing a child into an already stressed situation that had been complicated enough with just the two of us.

As much as I wanted to forgive Derrick, I found it hard to forget." I explained

I continued, "As part of our healing, I demanded that Derrick get tested. He assured me that he did not have any sexually transmitted diseases, but the truth was that he had slept with a random chic, and I myself without protection. He needed to be checked out. I would go with him to his appointment. I wanted to make sure that we addressed all of my concerns and see if there was any reason for the possible blackouts, emotional rollercoaster rides, and weird outbursts of anger. I wanted answers, and I was hopeful that seeing a doctor might shed some light on Derrick's behavior. "

"How do you think Derrick was feeling at this point? Did you give any consideration to his feelings about him aborting his child?" Dr. Mary quizzed.

"Fuck Derrick and his feelings" I calmly stated, taking a sip of water and looking her dead in the eyes through the computer screen.

I went on to add, "Derrick hadn't shown one bit of interest in my feelings."

Why do you think that?" Dr. Mary asked.

"Because I just found out that Derrick and Jessica's son is seven years old now. It seems that ole' Jessica had a change of heart about the abortion. Derrick kept this from me. He had been paying child support to Jessica for the past seven years" I divulged in an irritated tone.

Dr. Mary's look on her face said it all. She was as shocked as I was. There was a long pause as we both searched for words of affirmation.

"Not what you were expecting to hear?" I questioned. "Yes, it appears that Derrick had plenty of secrets. I gave birth to my child at six months. I got to hold him in my arms for all of five minutes as I said my goodbyes. Derrick's son was still alive.

And to make matters worse, Jessica recently died of Cancer. As the only surviving family member and executive for Derrick's estate, I am asked to either take their son in or sign him over to the state for foster care. Ain't this about some shit?" I disclosed to the still shocked doctor.

"What will you do Tracy?" Dr. Mary asked.

"I'm not sure. It appears that the child doesn't even know who Derrick is. According to the lawyer Derrick hired to oversee the child's financial needs, Derrick never had any physical contact with him. But now that Jessica is dead too, someone, Me, has to either become his guardian or forfeit my rights and give him to the estate" I confessed.

The alarm on Dr. Mary's phone went off, signaling the end of our session for the day, but we continued to talk through some things. I had more questions than I did answers. The only person that could help me understand was dead. But if I knew Derrick, there had to be little breadcrumbs to follow for explaining everything that was happening now. I just needed to start looking.

The Past

Derrick and I finally were at a point of pushing through this mess that he created. The doctor confirmed that Derrick did not have any STD's and that he was HIV negative. However, the doctor was concerned about the blackouts, memory loss, emotional highs and lows, and the bouts of anger that Derrick was enduring. He asked about his family medical history, of which Derrick couldn't answer the mental health questions for sure. Next, the doctor questioned what usually triggers some of these events and even asked for my input. Derrick and I could not agree on the possible causes that could set him off. Derrick had one version of accounts, and I gave another. Either way, we gave the doctor enough information to understand the frustration we both were going through in the recent months.

The doctor recommended that Derrick see another doctor who specializes in mental health. In the meantime, he arranged for Derrick to have a CT Scan of his brain to rule out any tumors or other possible issues that could be causing these impromptu behavioral issues. He handed us some literature on mental health. He gave Derrick a list of questions he may want to ask his mother and father before meeting with the specialist. I was not completely satisfied. I wasn't leaving with the answer I wanted today, but at least we were on the right road. I could sense that Derrick was not fully relieved of the uncertainty either.

In the meantime, I had allowed Derrick to join me for my prenatal OBGYN visits. He was able to hear the baby's heartbeat and see him dancing inside me. It was a brief moment of joy that we shared. I had almost forgotten that my first year of marriage had been tried, tested, and I was in no way winning the battle. At least not yet. It made Derrick smile, which was something I neglected to see in the past few weeks. Derrick always took the entire day off to spend with me whenever I had a doctor's appointment. He would turn the day into an event. He would go out of his way to make me feel special. It was mostly an overkill of gestures, but it made me relax and let down my guard just enough for me to see that he was trying.

The day had finally arrived for the visit with the mental health specialist. Derrick was nervous just as I was too. He had asked his parents about the mental health of their respective sides of the family. They were very vague in the answers. Either they honestly didn't know, or Derrick hadn't made it clear as to why he was asking. Their analysis of who in the family was crazy and who wasn't was comical, but not so much informative. This left Derrick and I still at first base. We were not anywhere closer to understanding what was happening with Derrick than when we started. We both were hoping the specialist would be able to shed some light on things today. Best case scenario, nothing was wrong with Derrick and he was just full of shit, but something told me there was more to his behavior than that.

The receptionist greeted Derrick and me. He had Derrick fill out the standard paperwork, signature and date. Within a few minutes, we were called back to see the doctor. The doctor explained what he hoped to gain from the appointment today. He asked if we had any questions before we got started. We both answered no. The doctor asked Derrick a series of questions, then he asked me to allow him and Derrick a moment to speak alone. I nodded and returned to the waiting room. About thirty minutes later, Derrick joined me. About ten minutes later, the doctor called us back into his office. He had completed his assessment of Derrick, and we were ready to hear what his diagnosis was.

The Present

A week had passed, and I wasn't feeling any better. The stress of Derricks's death hugged me like a sackcloth, and the news of his bastard child stung like rose thorns wrapped around my heart. I was not as cold hearted as this situation would have me be. I loved children. Hell, I wanted one of my own. I just don't want that kid. That child is a constant reminder of what Derrick did. I do not give a fuck if he was not in his right mind, crazy as fuck, or insane. He betrayed my trust, love, and marriage by sleeping with that bitch. But the more I looked at that child's picture, the more I longed for my own child. The more he favored Derrick. The more I needed Derrick here with me. Even now with his lie looming over me, I needed him, and I needed to know what he would want me to do.

I was staying busy with packing up Derrick's home office. I had dumped the file the attorney had given me and the boxes from his office at work right at the end of the staircase. I was moving the boxes and files to the basement when a stack of letters fell from the envelope that the attorney had given me. The bundled group of white envelopes were addressed to me. They all were written in Derrick's handwriting. Why am I just seeing this? I thought to myself. Did I forget something in my conversation with David that he had mentioned the letters, and I just could not recall? Either way, I had found them. My heart sank at the thought of what Derrick could have possibly needed to say in a letter that he could not share with me in person. I wanted to know. I wanted to know what was so important that even from the grave, he had something to say to me.

I dropped what I was doing, headed to our bedroom, closed the door, and there, I opened the first letter that Derrick had addressed to me. It read:

Dearest Red, (which was my nickname he had given me because of my reddish-brown hair color.)

If you are reading this, I know that you're upset at me for leaving you. I can't say for sure what may have happened that caused my absence, but I need you to know that I love you more than any words could express. You have been the light in my heart since the first time I held your hand that evening in the courtyard on campus. I knew right there that you would be my wife. That I would spend the rest of my days making you happy.

Well, it appears that I may have failed you. Not deliberately, but the moment I found out that I suffered from bipolar depression and personality disorder, things have never been the same between you and me. Your eyes used to shine like stars in the night, but when you found out that I was going have a child with someone else, your light dimmed.

If I could take my actions back, I would, just to see you smile again. Maybe if I would have paid attention to the signs and gotten diagnosed sooner than later. Perhaps I would have taken medicine that would have allowed me to continue to be the man you needed me to be. All I can offer are maybes. The fact is, I cannot excuse my behavior. What I know is that I hurt you. The doctor said I was unaware of my actions, that I wasn't in control of the part of my mind that distinguishes right from wrong. I say bullshit. I should have known. I should have been able to tell that she was not you. I should have been able to think through my actions, walked away, come home, and loved you. But we both know that was not the case.

I wanted to spend the rest of my life making it up to you, but my mind won't allow me to love you right between the guilt and the pain. Every night I hold you in my arms and every night I feel you pulling away from me. My body aches for your touch that has been absent from me for what seems like years. My biggest fear has been realized from the moment you found out I was not perfect. I wanted to be the god you prayed for and not the poor excuse of a mortal I had become. The hero that saved the day and gave you countless reasons to smile. Unfortunately, my cape was defective, my superhero powers were limited to my emotions, mental confusion and stagnant thoughts, and blackouts.

I wanted to love you, but my alter ego said I could not. It misled you into thinking the worst of me. He characterized me as an average nigga. One that could not be faithful, could not love, would not commit, nor would treat you like the queen you are to me. Me and him fought often. There were battles I would win, and days I lost. I was at war with the very part of me that needed you the most. The part of me that, had I allowed you to see me for who I was, had I allowed you to help me get through those rainy days, I would have weathered the storm and calmed the voice inside me that told me I wasn't worthy of you. But please know that I fought for you. I fought for us even though there was no chance in hell they would let me win. The victory was knowing that even if it was just a short part of my life, you loved me unconditionally in the beginning. Hopefully, as you read this letter and those that follow, you'll love me just a little while longer.

You are my nebulous and the power behind my existence. The sun at the end of my tunneled mind of clouds and mixed thoughts. The sun that brightens my ego and tears down those negative walls of mental anguish. Your touch calms my crazy and caresses my soul. You are the peace that allows me to focus and contain the chaos that resides within me. I prayed daily that despite my behavior, comments, and emotional rants, you knew this. And because my words neglected to reach you in kindness, I knew this letter would.

I love you Tracy Montgomery, and I hope these letters show you the many ways that I did and bring closure to my absence.

Derrick

The Past

I cannot lie, the news from the psychotherapist stunned both Derrick and myself. I had assumed depression may have plagued Derrick, but never had I thought I'd hear the words the doctor uttered. We had questions, concerns, and a slew of emotions that needed to be handled. How could we not know? How did I not see this? How could this be? What about my unborn child? Would he also be prone to this disease? We sat there together as the doctor began to explain Derrick's condition. With every detailed characteristic, behavior, and trait, the doctor painted a picture of Derrick in a reality that I was living. From his emotional outburst, the rollercoaster ride of highs and extreme lows, the nights he couldn't sleep and the desperate attempts for attention. The mood swings, the forgetfulness, the days he didn't seem like the man I had come to love and know. The fights, the arguments, and words he spoke but couldn't take back and wake up the next day as if nothing happened. All of it was starting to make sense. Without knowing, the doctor had just painted the pain of my existence that I had covered up for fear of failing and becoming a statistic. I had become blind to the facts that Derrick had something horribly wrong; something that was out of my control and apparently his. It was bigger than I could have imagined, and bigger than Derrick could admit.

Derrick sat there dazed, grasping for answers to combat his denial. Gripping my hand like a child holding on to his mother, I could see the fear in his eyes. I could see Derrick clearly for the first time. He wasn't a mad man, he wasn't an egocentric asshole, or a forgetful husband. He was a man in pain, hurting from the conflict within, and not having an outlet or any direction as to why. He was my perfectly imperfect husband. Now that I knew what was alienating him from me, I could love him even more. I had to. What else could I do? This was the part of the vows that married people hoped would never come—that part of for better or worse. We often lived in the better, maybe even bad, but never prayed for the worse. I had to show Derrick that I was here for him. That this did not change anything between us. That I was here for the long haul, committed for life as I had promised. I squeezed his hand back as we locked eyes and simultaneously, tears fell from our eyes. We were in this together.

The doctor shared with Derrick what his next steps would be. There would be therapy sessions, medication, journaling, and support groups to help us. But most of the work fell upon Derrick. It was his battle to fight. I could support and comfort, but this journey was his. As the passenger on this ride, all I could do was watch from the sidelines and cheer him on. The doctor told us that Derrick's disorder was manageable. But he needed to follow the regimen. We quickly filled up the doctor's calendar with appointments to begin Derrick's therapy. He handed Derrick a leather-bound journal and stylish pen.

"Today is the first day of you knowing about your disorder. Your demon will try with everything it has to derail you. If you allow me to help you, we can conquer it. You can control I, and you can live a normal happy life Derrick. Start writing your thoughts down from today. We went over a lot of information. It's ok to be angry, it's ok to be confused, it's alright to doubt what you've heard today. But what you can't do now that you know, is pretend that you don't know. It's the most dangerous thing you can do to yourself, your wife, and your unborn child" the doctor spoke with urgency.

Derrick rubbed my belly to acknowledge that he was willing to do what needed to be done to be here for us. I grinned a half smile at his gesture.

'I'm ready Doc." Derrick sighed and courageously spoke.

"That's what we want to hear Derrick. I will see you on Thursday. In the meantime, write your thoughts down. It will help you learn to process your feelings and behaviors more productively." The doctor stated firmly as he shook Derrick's hand and smiled at me to ease my worries.

Little did I know this would be the beginning of the end of a long journey of the true meaning of love, sacrifice, heartache, and pain. In good times and in bad times, for better or worse, would come to bruise me in ways I could not imagine. I had no idea the impact mental illness could have on a person. Not just the person fighting the battle, but those of us that stand by their side; those loving them in their darkest hour. I was about to learn just how unequipped my naïve heart was. Till death do us part should be stricken from the vows because when it happens, you are no more apart than you were together, and often left with unbearable sorrow that can't be wished away or left for time to heal. It just is.

The Present

I sat there numb as the streams of emotion covered me in joy and sorrow. I took solace in Derrick's words. I knew he loved me. I knew he cared. I also knew that I shared him with his inner demons. I knew that the man I loved and married would never, could never, be the person who showed up in this marriage most days. With his tortured soul fighting so hard to have a presence in my life. And how wonderful it was when I saw him. If even for a moment when the sunrays from the morning light would cascade through our bedroom window, and I could see the Derrick I knew as the light illuminated his perfect molasses color skin. The one who held me in his arms and whispered sweet nothings in my ear. The one who had mastered how to touch me and not leave a scar, the man that held me on a pedestal giving me the title of queen, the man who showered our kingdom with precious moments of amber and clay. I saw him in the smallest of moments, even when he wasn't looking.

I knew he loved me. I heard his voice whispering to me as if he were right in the room with me. I missed him in ways I never thought possible. I would take back all the hurtful exchanges, the doubt, the spiteful array of thought that echoed in my mind when Derrick did less than what I needed him to. I would forgive every second that he irked my soul. I would freely tolerate his shortcomings and allow myself to love him without judgement. His words spoke to me his real thoughts and how selfish I must have been. How self-centered I must have been to be so reckless with his fragile heart. Now I sit alone, wondering what I could have done differently. Instead of crying myself asleep and calling out for him without an answer, I wonder if things were different, would I be laying in the warmth of his arms, possibly hearing his sweet voice whispering in my ear.

I allowed myself to feel the emotions that hung over me like a cloud following the sky. I had hardened my heart to the disorder that had come to plague my marriage and refused to cope with the reality that I wasn't the only one hurting. As much as Derrick tried, he was fighting a war he could not win. I had promised to be there for him in his worse moments. Somewhere along the way, I had forgotten what that meant. I had given up on us. I chose to cover up and mask the disorder to protect what I thought was our happy life. The only person I fooled was myself. There were signs I am sure that Derrick had issues that needed attention, I think we all chose to ignore them. I decided to ignore them. Hiding them in the back of the closet wrapped up tight in a pretty package so no one would know. I knew. And that should have been enough for me to hold on tighter, wrap my arms around him and not let go. I should have had the strength to force him to open his eyes and see what was right here in front of him, instead of forcing him to console his unreliable thoughts and feelings. I knew, and how I wish I could tell him now, how sorry I am for not loving him enough. That I do! That I do need you!

"Oh Derrick, I love you!" I cried aloud.

The silence of the house absorbed my cries. I felt him in the room with me. That was all that mattered. He was here, and I needed to hear more from him. I counted the letters. There were ten altogether. Ten letters for me to understand the man fighting for his existence to belong in a world he had no control of. I needed to know him. I wanted to know him. I tried to pretend that we were back in college, laughing and joking. I wanted to see the way I caught him looking at me in the quiet moments we shared. I wondered if he still... I wondered if in the moments he was fighting the conflicts in his mind, did he think of those happier days. I wanted to tell him I did. I do and will always remember him that way. I wrapped myself up in Derrick's bathrobe, and the smell of his cologne choked me as I breathed him in. I sat there with his final words to me, and I knew without reading them that he loved me. He loved me in the darkest moments, even in the fights, external and internal; Derrick wanted me to know he cared.

The Past

———— ❧ ————

At first, Derrick seemed optimistic about his diagnosis. He was journaling daily. He willingly took his medication, and he never missed an appointment with his therapist. It was a routine that I could clock as if to tell time. Derrick seemed happy. His mood swings, emotional ups and downs all leveled out. I saw glimmers of the old Derrick. It was almost like we were back to normal. I had even made the conscious decision to forgive Derrick. After knowing now what he was battling, how could I hold a grudge? His disorder clearly had led Derrick to act in manners that he normally would not. Things were looking up in the Montgomery house. Both Derrick and I wore our smiles with Pride, or so it appeared.

My belly was steadily growing. Derrick would leave work early to join me for my OBGYN appointments. The smile on his face made my heart melt. Every week we would shop for our little boy's clothing. Derrick thought of our son as his mini me. He would always pick out matching outfits and hats. I would laugh and allow him to buy whatever he wanted to. After all, this was the bright side of our lives. If it gave Derrick a bright spot and something to look forward to, I was all for it. We would end our day by having a romantic dinner out. We enjoyed The Union located downtown Kalamazoo. It became our go-to spot as most of the foods I craved were on their menu.

Derrick would also have something up his sleeve. He made a habit of surprising me with lavish gifts. I would tell him that he already won me. He would laugh and give me a playful wink.

"Tracy, I want to keep winning at loving you. I never want you to feel like I take you for granted. I could never show you enough or say it enough, but I love you girl; you mean everything to me. So, if I spoil you, it's because I want to, because you deserve it." He said with a confidence I had missed about him.

We ended the night by making love and enjoying each other in ways that reminded me why I loved him so. His touch sent chills up and down my body. After years, I still got the same rush of nervousness when he entered me. He stroked me tenderly and caressed my body. He had mastered the art of knowing me. I would look into his pretty brown eyes and see my reflection. Every moan meant he had explored yet another part of my body he could lay claim to. I had wished for him in my dreams and every time we made love, I was reminded how God answers prayers. We made good ole fashion love. The kind of love that inspired songs, the kind of love that babies were conceived. It was the music that filled our house as I cried out in my soprano vocatives when he strung my strings, and he complimented my tones with his baritone moans.

There wasn't anything that I would not do for Derrick. I loved him like no one before him. The way my tongue traveled along his spine and tickled the veins in his manhood was so much that it got him excited in ecstasy. The way he poured his soul into me, the way he tenderly held me as I rode his thrusts, with all the twist, turns, sucking and moans, we gave each other the best parts of ourselves in that moment. It was pure, honest and genuine. We were our authentic selves, flaws and all.

I would lay in Derrick's arms and listen to his heartbeat. It was the tone that controlled my breathing and relaxed my soul. I felt safe again. It felt like home. It was days and nights like this that made me believe that we could stay in this moment forever. It was the "better" in my vows, the health before the sickness that was to come. What I did not know was days like this would become less and rarer. Not necessarily the sex, but the security. The feeling of being loved on both our parts and the calmness that captured the peace and harmony of our love. So, I held him just a little tighter that night. Not knowing why, but I just did. Every chance I got, I told him I loved him. I whispered it in his ear that night. He smiled and kissed me on my forehead. It was the best sleep I had ever had.

The Present

I had shared with Dr. Mary the letters I had found from Derrick. We discussed how I felt, my reactions, and how I was coping with his absence. I had to admit, I was starting to move forward. I no longer felt stuck. Sure, I was angry sometimes, I cried on many days, but I was okay at the end of it all. Every day became a little easier to navigate. The constant reminders of Derrick that surrounded me in the house became prized possessions instead of annoyances that I wanted to rid myself of. I had never noticed before how much love lived in our home. I had concentrated on the bad memories when in comparison, the good memories outweighed and outnumbered them.

Derrick's depression and mental illness was not the only stain on our marriage. I began to see the role I played in tearing down the very foundation I prayed be strengthen. My words were not always kind. I had forgotten how to speak in love to my husband. I worshipped his flaws and neglected to see his fruits. I was so fixated on catching him not doing something that I failed to see how my behavior projected my own insecurities on him. Not only was I oblivious to his needs, but I abandoned my marriage emotionally and left him to fend for himself in his most fragile state.

I did not realize the woman I claimed to be and the works of the woman I had become were not the same. I wanted to point out that Derrick did not take his medicine every time he skipped a therapy session. If my words were a two-edged sword, certainly, I have killed him over and over again. I wished I had known what I knew now. I wonder if it would have made a difference for Derrick. I wonder if he would still be here now. It could not have been tolerable fighting me, himself and the demons that reside in his mind. He was never gonna win every battle.

Dr. Mary stated that she was proud of my progress. Although the sessions were still virtual, I felt the sincerity in Dr. Mary's voice. I also saw the change in me. I could finally raise my head and look her in the eyes of the laptop camera. Plus, I was bathing regularly. I laughed to myself.

I think I had Derrick to thank for that. I had started to see that he did not leave me, at least not in the way I had blamed him for. He was battling something, unfortunately, that I hope I'll never know. Something bigger than him, more powerful than the love I could give, and pain so unbearable that it hurt to live. I knew that he was at peace now. I also knew that he still loved me even if he wasn't here physically. I smiled, knowing that he does not have to fight anymore. That the only battle left for him to endure is waiting for me to join him in death. And as much as I long to see and be with him, we will both have to wait on time and God for that.

After today's session, I had an actual doctor's appointment with my primary doctor. I still was not feeling my best. It was not the symptoms of Covid-19, but because it's been a few weeks, I wanted to make sure it wasn't some other harmful virus. I arrived at my doctor's office off of Center Street. The waiting room was sparsely populated. The social distancing made it feel almost abandoned because the seats were so spread apart. I had my choice of any number of open seats. Everywhere you looked, there were postings on social distancing, the importance of washing your hands, wearing a mask, and staying home if you can. For me, this all made sense. Besides, where was I going or who did I have to be around? Absolutely no one. And maybe for now, that was the best thing for me. I needed this time to clear my mind and get right with myself.

The young woman dressed in scrubs opened the door that leads to the examination rooms that lined the hallway.

"Tracy, Dr. Thatcher will see you now" her cheery voice sang out loud.

I immediately stood up and followed her down the hall into examination room four. She completed the formality checks of my vitals. With all the stress, I had managed to lose fifteen pounds. I was sure that Dr. Thatcher would have plenty to say about that. Blood pressure was normal, but I did have a slight fever. I was given the hospital gown to dress into. Within minutes, there was a knock at the door, and in walked Dr. Thatcher. Dr. Thatcher was a petite Asian woman whose presence commanded attention. She had been my doctor ever since I had made Michigan home. I had grown very fond of Dr. Li Xui Thatcher. We both had similar stories of womanhood that we both shared. And our pursuit of success outside of our husbands' careers both propelled us on a path to create our own destiny, carving out lives for ourselves.

"Tracy, my favorite patient, how are you doing my dear" Dr. Thatcher hugged me as she entered the room.

"Better" I politely replied.

"Cut the bullshit, Tracy. I know you like a mother knows her daughter. Really, how are you my friend?" She dug a little deeper with her questioning.

"I feel like shit. But everyone wants me to smile. I am not ready to be around people, so thank god for this pandemic. I'm seeing a therapist; I think the shit is helping and all I do is cry to myself. I miss my husband and all his crazy ass ways. I'm alone because I want to be right now, and I think I shouldn't be. And I'm hoping you can tell me if I have a fucking cold, flu or whatever that's curable because right now I don't think I could take another piece of bad news." I blurted out in one breath.

"Well shit lady, that was a lot" Dr. Thatcher jokingly said.

I smiled as I opened my mouth for her to view my tonsils. She looked into my ears, rolled her fingers across my glands and listened to my heartbeat. She paused and took a step back.

"What?" I asked, concerned.

"When was the last time you had your menstrual cycle?" She quizzed.

"I... I don't know. I've been under so much stress... I haven't given it any thought. Why? Why are you asking me that? What's wrong with me? I demanded to know.

"Calm down Tracy. I think you're pregnant." She calmly stated.

"WHAT THE FUCK!" I screamed out loud.

She just shook her head to motion yes.

She handed me a cup for a urine sample and pointed to the door. "Go!" she commanded.

I marched out of the room and down the hall. I was shocked. My mind started racing. Could I be? How did this happen? I wondered to myself.

I collected the urine, wiped off the cup, sealed it tight, washed my hands, and rushed back to the room. Dr. Thatcher was already waiting for me. She wheeled in portable ultrasound equipment, and the nurse was waiting with her. I handed off the specimen cup and laid it down on the examination table. The nurse shook her head and Dr. Thatcher smiled. "Just as I suspected, you're going to be a mommy" she smiled. "Now, let's see how far long you are" she continued. Within seconds I could hear the fast-paced heart echoes of someone inside of me. The screen painted an abstract view of my womb, and there, right there was my baby, Derrick's baby.

Dr. Thatcher moved the wand around, capturing the various measurements of my unborn baby. All along, the tears flowed down my cheek. I was pregnant, and the only thing I wanted to do was run and tell Derrick. Celebrate with him, but he was no longer here for me to do that with him. I didn't know how to respond. I just laid there focused on the view, the images of something so beautiful, something I wasn't expecting, the last gift from my husband, a piece of him that I had longed for all these months and here it was. I felt so alive. I felt so loved. I felt complete in even this moment of sadness.

Dr. Thatcher had announced that I was 16 weeks pregnant. I could not believe it. There were only a few times before Derrick's death that we had sex. The one time that stands out was a few days before his death. He seemed so happy and at peace. It was almost like I had my husband back. We had made love like we had so many times before, but it felt different. It felt like the first time. I had hoped that it would have last forever. But the next morning, I woke up and Derrick had transitioned into the stranger I had come to know. It was three days later that he took his life. Even in the madness, Derrick left me something so special. I wondered if he planned it that way. I wondered if he knew that I would need someone to love and a part of him to help me move on and always remember him by.

The Past

It had been three solid months since finding out about Derrick's condition. I remember thinking about how good things had been. Derrick seemed like he was calm and had come to grips with living with his diagnosis. I mean, he went to work every day with a smile on his face. He returned home and was a loving and supportive husband. We ate dinner together every day. I'd lay in his arms every night. He would read books and sing to my baby bump. We were just starting to relax into our marriage life. We had so far conquered what had been thrown at us. We were living our dreams out loud, and things finally felt normal.

It was a Thursday. I remember because I had a doctor's appointment. I waited for Derrick in the usual spot in the parking lot. We would usually drive separate cars and then drop off one of the cars at home and spend the rest of the afternoon doing whatever felt good. My appointments were usually around two o'clock in the afternoon. I waited fifteen minutes for Derrick, but he did not show. I tried calling and texting him, but there was no reply. I figured that he must have gotten busy at work. Occasionally there were emergency meetings for high profile clients. I wasn't going to worry too much.

The doctor gave me a clean bill of health and our baby boy was doing great. His heartbeat was normal. My measurements were right where they needed to be. I was entering my sixth month of pregnancy. I was really starting to show. Derrick thought it was so cute how my body was transforming. From my breast to my hips. Everything seemed so enhanced and accentuated. Derrick would run his fingers over my curves when he held me at night. He would always stop and kiss my belly and tell our son how much he loved him already. It was moments like that that I looked forward to. The doctor gave me an updated picture of our growing baby. I couldn't wait to share it with Derrick.

I left the doctor's office. I checked my phone before driving off, but there was no message, no texts. I dismissed it because, like I said, he could have gotten busy. I would share with him the good news later tonight at dinner. Before heading home, I ran to the mall. The Children's Place was having a sale. I wanted to look around and start buying clothes in some of the bigger sizes. I had already begun to shop for baby clothes in sizes 0-12 months. I had everything from layettes, onesies, one-piece joggers set, baby Nike, sweatsuits, and of course, the matching outfits that Derrick had purchased. The only thing this kid was missing was shoes. I was sure that once he was born, Derrick would make sure they had that in common too.

I was happy that I stopped by the mall. I was able to get a lot of the items I was looking for. By the time I had left the mall, it was close to six o'clock. I guess it's true what they say about shopping, time flies when you're having fun. I checked my phone. There was nothing from Derrick still. No worries. I would just order dinner and head home. I pulled into the garage and there was Derrick's car. I was sure after the long day he had today, he would be hungry and tired. I grabbed my bags and headed into the house. I put the bags down at the back door. I called out for Derrick, but there was no answer. I went to the bedroom, but he was not there. I thought maybe he was washing the days stress away. I walked around the entire house, but no Derrick. I noticed the patio door was unlocked. Looking out, I could see him sitting with his back toward me. He had his Beats headset on. That would explain why he hadn't replied to me calling out for him.

I walked out onto the patio. I wrapped my arms around him and kissed him on the cheek. His reaction was not what I was expecting. There was a startled jump. He turned to look at me. It was then that I could tell that something was off. I didn't want to jump to conclusions. But I knew. I had seen that look before.

"Hey Derrick," I cautiously said.

He had been drinking. I had noticed the emptied bottles of Hennessy next to him. He didn't respond right away. He just sat there looking me up and down. His eyes were off. I took a deep breath and replayed everything the therapist had said that Derrick needed to do to help him manage his disorders. Drinking was not on the list; in fact, it did not go well with the medication he was on.

"Derrick, are you hungry honey?" I asked

"Where the fuck you been?" he interrupted me before I could tell him what I had picked up to eat. His eyes. His eyes.

"Derrick, don't you remember, I had a doctor's appointment. You were supposed to meet me there." I commented.

"That's right," he said smiling. "How is my baby boy doing?" he continued as he sipped from the glass of brown liquor.

"It went well, I have a new picture for you" I added. "Why don't we go inside to eat and then talk. You can tell me all about your day and I'll fill you in on mine" I gestured as I began to walk away.

"Tracy, get your ass back here!" he screamed out.

The tone of his voice startled me. I turned and faked a smile. "Derrick, I'm hungry baby, I really need to eat" I responded. I lied. I had lost my appetite. I just wanted to get away from him. I wasn't sure what was going on, but Derrick was not himself. I wasn't sure if I needed to call his therapist or allow Derrick to explain what happened. The scary thing is I wasn't sure he was in a position to defend himself. I just wanted to create some space so I could breathe. His tone, his demeanor, everything about him made me feel uncomfortable. Especially his eyes. I walked with a quickened pace back into the house. I prayed he didn't follow.

I found my cell phone. I searched my contacts and found Derrick's therapist number. I quickly dialed it. The call went to voicemail.

"Dr. David, this is Tracy Montgomery. I was hoping I could talk to you about Derrick. Something seems off with him. I'm not sure if there is a new medication he is trying or if he had a bad session. Can you please call me back? Thank you." I ended the call.

"Who the fuck you calling? I thought you said you were so hungry. Why the fuck you on the phone and not sitting down eating?" he questioned.

"It was nothing Derrick." I whispered.

I walked around the kitchen island, grabbed a plate, and began to unpack the food I brought home. I fixed my plate, while Derrick watched my every move. I sat down and ate the room temperature food. Derrick just stared at me in silence. I finished my plate, rinsed off the plate, and fork, then placed them in the dishwasher. I unpacked the food and placed the uneaten portions in the refrigerator. I walked by Derrick, Kissed him on the cheek. I made my way to the bedroom, closed the door and cried.

That night I slept uneasily. I also slept alone. Derrick never made it to bed. I was thankful that he hadn't. I almost went to get a drink of water in the middle of the night, but I could hear him yelling and talking to himself when I opened the bedroom door. I closed the door and climbed back into bed. I prayed he didn't hear me. The last thing I wanted was for us to argue tonight. I didn't have the energy, and I didn't want to escalate whatever was happening with him to a new level.

The following morning, I slowly walked downstairs. There was no sign of Derrick. I figured he had finally crashed and would be sleeping on the couch or in his office. But he was gone and so was his car. He left a trail of damage behind. There were broken glasses, whiskey-soaked papers on the floor, and empty alcohol bottles scattered all around the house. I cleaned up what I could. I called the cleaning service and asked for an off scheduled full cleaning of the house. Within an hour, a staff of four members of Molly Maids was at my door. And just as quickly as they had arrived, they had cleaned are were gone. While they cleaned, I began emptying all the alcohol in the house. I cleaned out the bar, the guest room bar, the kitchen over stock and the bar in his office. I poured it all down the drain. I took the emptied bottles to the recycle container. I then locked the cabinets of the bar and hid the keys.

I tried working. My mind was certainly not focused on contacting clients. Cause I was stressed and worried. I wanted to know what was going on with Derrick. Last night came out of nowhere. It was almost like he had never been to therapy like he had not been taking his medicine. I could not make sense of any of this. Wherever Derrick was, I was hoping that he would be in a much better mood when he returned and be willing to talk things through.

Derrick arrived home on time as usual. He had gone to work like nothing had happened. He entered the house in an upbeat manner. He was all smiles and carrying flowers. He walked right over to me and kissed me on my cheek before I had an opportunity to pull away. He smelled like saturated cologne and cigar smoke, which was weird because he didn't smoke. He winked at me a flashed those lying dimples that I had now come to resent.

"Oh, I almost forgot," he gestured for me to wait a moment as he rushed back into the garage. He came back into the house carrying the stuffed elephant that I had wanted to get for the nursey. It had a big bow wrapped around the elephants' neck. Under any other circumstances, this would have made my day. I just smiled a half grin and whispered thank you. Derrick was so pleased with his act of kindness that he was oblivious to me reaction.

I decided to lay down for a little while. At least I knew that he was home safe and sound. I must have been sleeping for about an hour before I heard the blaring sounds of music coming up the stairs. I hurried downstairs to see what was going on. There in the middle of his own chaos, was Derrick. Dancing and singing at the top of his lungs. He was his one-person party. I tried to walk away before he saw me, but it was too late. He reached for me, grabbing my hand and pulled me into him to join in the festivities. I had become an unwilling participant in his dance party. He began to sing in my ear in a tone-deaf array of melodies. I was more annoyed than impressed. As soon as the song was over, I gracefully bowed out. I took my exit and ran.

Derrick called after me. I motioned just to wait a moment as I headed back upstairs. I closed the bedroom door behind me and took a deep breath. I didn't know what was happening. Why was he behaving so erratically? I sat on the bed, trying to figure out what was going on. My cell phone buzzed to signal a missed call or text message. I recognized the number. It was Derrick's therapist. I immediately listened to the message that he left me.

"Mrs. Montgomery, thank you for reaching out to me. Unfortunately, I do not have answers for you. Derrick called me a few days prior to our first session, and he cancelled. He stated that he would be seeking assistance from another therapist. I wished him well and told him to let me know if there was anything I could do to help. He didn't give me a name, so I can't refer you to the new doctor. I'm a little concerned with your message. Please call me if there is anything I can do." The doctor concluded the message.

My heart sunk deep inside of me. I held back the tears. He's been lying to me all this time. He said that everything was going well. I saw him writing in his journal every night before bed. I saw him writing. I reached over to Derrick's nightstand. I opened the journal. I could not believe what I was reading. Page after page, Derrick wrote the same words over and over again. There were pages with nothing but the phrase "NOT ME" penned. The tears rolled down my face. I could feel the instant shock of betrayal sweep over me. For months, he sat here and wrote this. I immediately jumped up and ran to the bathroom. I opened the medicine cabinets took the medication that his therapist prescribed and opened the bottles. I counted each bottle. They all had the original pill count that was prescribed. I then opened the daily pill container. The tears flowed even faster down my face. I started to sob uncontrollably as I looked inside the pill container. Derrick had filled it with aspirin, vitamins and some kind of supplement. He had not taken one day of medication. He wasn't seeking help, and the drug I thought was helping was just Derrick pretending. He had played me. And I fell for it.

I called the therapist back right away after my discovery. He answered on the second ring.

"Dr. Winston, thank you so much for returning my call." I spoke up as soon as he answered.

"Mrs. Montgomery, no worries. Once I heard your message, I became very worried. Please, tell me what is going on with Derrick?" he asked.

I began to explain to Dr. Winston Derrick's behavior over the past few days. He asked if that was the first episode since we last saw him. I had to think back over the past three months. I paused. There were signs and red flags as I recalled some of Derrick's behavior. More tears rolled down my already stained face. I continued to fill Dr. Winston in on Derrick, his journal, and the medication.

"This is what I feared would happen. Derrick needs help. I'm concerned for your safety and his. Where is he now?" Dr. Winston quizzed.

"He's downstairs" I quickly replied.

"I'm on my way. I'll bring help. Stay upstairs. I fear that his personality disorder is spinning out of control. We might not be dealing with Derrick. This could explain his behavior. I won't know until I'm able to speak with him." He explained. "Text me your address; I'm calling for assistance. I'll be there in about fifteen minutes. We will get him the help he needs." Dr. Winston firmly stated.

I almost believed him. Just as I was hanging up the phone, Derrick walked in. He looked at the journal on the bed that was open to the scribbled pages. He saw the pill bottles of unused medication. I saw the anger cross his face. I knew that he knew I was on to him. There was nowhere for him to hide.

"What the fuck are you doing going through my stuff!" He yelled, grabbing the journal off the bed. "So, now you're checking up on me, huh!" he continued as he angrily pushed all the stuff off the bed.

"Derrick, listen, I'm just concerned about you, baby. I just wanted to make sure you're ok. I didn't..." I tried to explain.

"Concerned for me? What the fuck are you talking about? I told you I was fine." Derrick cried out.

"Derrick, you are not fine honey. I thought you were seeing your therapist?" I tried to continue.

"So you spoke to my therapist? You're spying on me now! Checking up on me?" He said as he grabbed me by my arm.

"Derrick let me go, please" I pleaded as he held me tight.

"Derrick, please, you need help baby. You can't control it. It's not your fault. You just can't do this by yourself." I tried rationalizing my behavior to him.

"You stupid bitch, you don't know shit. You and that doctor just want to control me. I told him and now I'm telling you, I DON'T NEED NO PILLS, OR THERAPY!" He yelled in my face.

"Derrick, you're hurting me! Let me go please!" I pleaded.

His grip on me grew stronger.

"I asked you to just dance with me, enjoy the moment and you're up here spying on me. You are just like everyone else. Do you think I don't know what you're up to? You think I haven't noticed the late nights that you come home. The way you have been dressing. You're the one changing; you're the one up to shit. It ain't me bitch, It's you!" He screamed as he threw me to the floor.

I fell backward and hit my head on the corner of the bed post.

Derrick started talking to himself, begging to stop, and pleading with someone that was not there. He started throwing stuff at the walls. I tried backing away from him. He threw the lamp that sat on my nightstand at the wall, breaking it on impact.

The tears wouldn't break from falling. It was the first time I had ever seen Derrick this upset. It was the first time he had ever put his hands on me. I wanted to believe that it wasn't him doing this, that he truly needed help. But the man in front of me looked every bit like Derrick. His voice, this face, his build. It was all him, but his eyes told a different story. I wasn't sure who those belonged to. The scary thing is, I had seen them before. Maybe too many times before and this was the first time they knew I knew I could see them clearly now.

Derrick and I locked eyes as I tried to get up and out of the room. It happened so fast, I didn't really have my balance. I was still a little dizzy from hitting my head on the bed post, but he was coming after me. I wasn't sure what he was going to do. I wasn't sure if it was Derrick or if it was the person behind the eyes, the one who had taken over my husband, the stranger that had resided in my house for the last few months. All I knew was I had to go. But before I knew what happen, I lost my balance. I felt myself slip, and I couldn't regain balance.

The Present

I couldn't sleep. I tried everything. A cup of chamomile tea, a hot bath, and I even meditated for a few minutes. Yet still, I was up at this late hour. I reached into my nightstand and grabbed the bundle of envelopes that were wrapped in order, just as Derrick placed them. I took the envelope opener and slid it along the creased top that had been secured tight. It was the second letter that Derrick had written. I wasn't sure if I wanted to read it, but my soul yearned to hear his voice. I needed to feel him here with me. It was the reason I was up and sleepless. I never slept well without Derrick, even when I was upset with him. As long as he was in the house, I was fine and could sleep.

"Dearest Tracy,

By now, I hope that you are adjusting to your new, new normal. I hope that the cure for COVID-19 is underway, that you and my mother are at peace, even with each other. Most importantly, I hope that you are sleeping well. (Even though I know that you aren't.) I'm sure if I'm fortunate to be watching over you, it would be because I miss you and need to make sure that you are moving on and living your life without worry.

I need to apologize for something. I wasn't sure how to bring this up without adding the memories you fought so hard to bury. I will never forgive myself for the night ... The night you fell and lost the baby. I blamed myself for it all. I played that night in my mind every day. I could've, should've, would've done anything to prevent that from happening. I tell myself I should have taken the medicines, gotten the therapy, not pushed you away, been a better husband, fought harder, did anything to prevent that night. But the truth is I can't. It had become the vein of my existence. My heart hadn't recovered after that night. No number of drugs or therapy would calm the thoughts and voices in my head. They were right, they were all right, I was not the man you needed me to be, and I never would be.

But you, you were so brave. I watched you give birth to our son, hold him in your arms and let him go with the grace of an angel. I sat there holding you while we said good-bye to our son, and I knew in my heart that you would not blame me for our misfortune but would find a way to try to forgive me. But I would not allow you to. That night that I held you in my arms was the last time I would willingly allow you to love me. I didn't deserve you. I didn't deserve the life you were trying to create for us. So, I just gave up. It didn't matter anymore. Nothing mattered. I had failed you in the worse way. I knew it, the voice inside of me agreed and for a while, your eyes told me as well.

I never apologized the way I thought you deserved it. I never was able to muster the courage to tell you how much of a coward I was. But I guess you know that by now. I wish there were a word that would qualify to subtract the immense amount of pain I've caused you. Lord knows I tried to get right to make you happy. But it would never be enough. Nothing I could offer would undo the web of pain I had cast on our marriage. All I have to offer is my sincerest apology and even that falls short because I couldn't do it in person. This was the only way I knew you would hear me and know that I mean it from the core of my being.

I don't think this will help you sleep tonight, but it should bring you a little peace knowing and closure. I never blamed you. I know why you ran, I never meant to scare you, hurt you or make you cry. I couldn't control that which resides inside me. I wish I could, I wish I had the black boy magic to make me the husband that could have killed the inner voices and protected you from the rash of trauma that plagued us. You will be a great mother one day. You were meant to play that role, even better than that of a wife. You'll do it without me there to be a blind spot to your future. You'll do it without worrying about whether or not I would compromise the process. You are an amazing woman, Tracy Montgomery. I was blessed to be able to call you my wife, and the mother of my child.

Good Night my sweet Tracy, and tell my sons I said I love them.

And Yes, I know.

The Past

A fter losing my baby, it became harder to put up with Derrick and live the lie that was our marriage. As I recalled the events that led up to my falling down the stairs, he may not have pushed me, but he certainly was the root for why I was fleeing. His unpredictable behavior had become too much for me to bear. Derrick agreed to seek professional help. And for a while, it helped. He attended therapy faithfully. I babysat him taking his medication. And like a prisoner in his own home, I counted the pills, inspected his mouth and checked his journal entries. Derrick agreed to all of it. But I wasn't sure this is what I signed up for in a marriage. This had become a one-sided partnership. I had given and taken more than anyone should expect to endure. I saw my life, marriage and husband slipping away like grains of sand.

Every day, Derrick tried to create the feelings that brought us together. The dinners, us attempting to communicate, watching TV together, all failed gestures in my heart to rekindle what was lost. I played along, but I knew he knew there was nothing he could do to undo the mistakes we both made thus far. I wasn't ready to hear his apologies, and he wasn't prepared to face the emotional burden his mental illness has placed on us. It was great that he sought the assistance he so desperately needed, but it couldn't be for me. It certainly wasn't for our son. It had to be because he wanted it, and I wasn't completely convinced that Derrick saw it that way. If he was motivated by guilt, then his efforts were soon to be spoiled by the reality that he would fail, yet again.

Derrick continued to work and come home like clockwork. We would meet at the door and enter our awkward existence of normal. I attended all of Derrick's work events. I smiled to disguise the sadness that had plagued my soul. I worked the room like an actress buying for the converted academy award nomination and would win at the cost of losing herself in the role. From the outside, I was put together. From the hair, my face, the clothes, the physique, but internally I had suffocated myself in the secret life of Derrick. No one knew. No one needed to. What advice, what words of acceptance, condolences, encouragement could you provide him or me? No one would understand the gravity of what he was pushing through. No one would readily walk a mile in his shoes for fear of being trapped in the solitude of depression or entertaining his inner self, only to be confused by the equally talented personalities that hunger for existence within him. No, no one needed to know. It saved us from the judgmental stares and glares for those too consumed by their own weak, pathetic lives.

Months went by. I played the role of wife for Derrick. It was, after all, what I had agreed to when I signed the marriage certificate. It was a badge of honor and respect that I had promised willingly to uphold. What should have been the easiest of hats to wear daily became my hardest struggle to maintain. He tried. Derrick was committed to being a better husband, a better person and conquering his mental illness. I complimented him on his efforts. I wanted him to be successful, I needed him to be. I wanted more than Derrick, the happily ever after I was promised as a little girl. I needed him to show me that he could be strong enough to conquer all that prevented him from giving his whole self to me. I needed to prove myself wrong, to prove that the works of my bleeding heart followed my faith in him, marriage, and God, was not in vain. Oh, how he tried. And the only thing I could give most days was a half-hearted smile and a kiss on the cheek.

It had been a year since that tragic night. I had made it through what I thought was hell and back. I had allowed Derrick to occupy room in my heart once again. His efforts began to win me over. Our dinners became more palatable. Our conversations more open, honest and loving. I was less drill sergeant in my approach with him and more like the college sweetheart, that would occasionally admire him from a distance when he wasn't looking. I even allowed myself to yearn for his touch. His eyes became the window to a future we could push toward. And those dimples, those dimples I loved once more. It felt good to see him again and to know that he saw me. We were slowly on the road to healing, forgiveness, and peace.

The Present

I woke up feeling relieved. Derrick's parting words in the letter I just read brought me a comforting peace. He knew, he knew I was pregnant. How did he know? I smiled. It also brought about more questions than answers. I needed to know what Derrick was thinking. His letters reached me in ways he could never communicate to me. Or was it that I was finally listening to him. Either way, I was thankful that he left these letters for me. Thankful that he knew how much I would need this.

I grabbed the stack of letters and headed downstairs to the kitchen. I poured myself a cup of tea laced with a swirl of lavender honey. I sat at the nook facing the bay window. The leaves are starting to change their colors again. 2020 had played a horrible game of Life for me. As unwilling a contestant, I had been, the hand that was dealt me continued to play itself. It was mornings like this that Derrick and I would call for a lazy Saturday. We would watch movies and enjoy each other's company. Put on some music and just party, just the two of us. It was days like today that brought back all the fun memories we shared. There were many, despite the nightmares we woke up to. I missed him.

I took the stack of envelopes and tore into the third letter. I sipped the hot tea and began to read Derrick's thoughts.

Dearest Tracy,

Good Morning, my sweet lady. I hope that you were able to rest finally. I know my last letter may have left you with more questions than answers. Well, let me see if I can shed some light on a few things for you. First, yes, I know you're pregnant. It made me smile with joy that you and I would be having another child. My only regret is that I would not be there with you to celebrate the joys of life with you. If I could be there with you, I would. I just could not take the chance that I would repeat history. Better yet, be the cause of any more pain for you. God forbid that I... I do anything again to cause you to lose another child. I just could not, would not endanger either one of you. Just know that this is one of the greatest moments in my life, next to marrying you.

You will be an awesome mother Tracy. I do not doubt this. And I trust that you will surround our child with all the love and security he needs. Yes, I'm hoping that the child you're carrying is a boy. Someone to carry on my name, someone that when you look at him, you'll be reminded of all the good I could have been. That you'll know how much I loved you. I know that you'll tell him just what kind of man I was. The good and the ugly. But you'll do it in such a way, that he'll be inspired by the man you wished I'd been. That he will grow up to do great things and make us both proud. I have nothing but confidence in the fact that you can and will do this.

Unfortunately, I also know that you are aware of the child that I had outside our marriage is still alive. I could not bring it to your attention. I found out shortly after we lost our child. She chose to keep the baby against my will. But I promised myself that I would never disrespect you ever again. So, I never saw him. I did set up an account for him. I did want to support him. So, I made sure that he didn't want for anything. Even though I wanted to, I couldn't be a part of his life. Not after I had hurt you the way I did. Not after knowing that my mental health was so unstable. I feared that I would hurt him too. So, I stayed away. I never even saw a picture of him. It was best that way. I was a coward on so many levels. But I wish I could have been a better man, father, husband for you all. I should've and would've, if it was in me. I hope you believe that.

I also know that his mother was dying from cancer and may have passed by now. I know I have no right to ask you for anything, but I am. I've given this a lot of thought, a way for everyone to heal. For me to undo all the wrong, I have done for allowing my mental illness to hurt so many. He needs you, just like our son needs you, just like our dear son Jackson did. He needs an opportunity to be loved and cared for by the only person I trust to do so. He deserves to know that his father wasn't a bad man, just a man who couldn't be the father he needed him to be. He deserves the right to carry my last name with honor just like our sons do. Not with the stigma, this world will place on them because of my absence. But you need him too. You need to learn to love again. Freely love and forgive. I know you have it in you. Your heart is too big not to. If you accept my son as yours, I'll know that you meant everything you've ever said to me. For better or worse, in good times and bad, your vows and mines finally at peace with everything that has happened in our marriage. The final act of love. Like I said, I don't have the right to ask, but I am. Be the mother he deserves to have. Something tells me he won't disappoint you. Just love him, like you loved me. That's a great place to start.

Whatever you decide, know I will always respect and love you. Tracy Montgomery, you are way stronger than you think. Your strength is one of the qualities I've always admired about you. That and your big ass heart! Find room for me, and my sons. We all need you. And you need us too.

Enjoy your day.

Loving you always,

Derrick

I sat there with a river of tears in my eyes. He had no right to ask. I hated him for it, and I love him even more in that moment for trusting me. My tea had gone cold and my heart was slowly warming up.

The Present

I was dressed. I had called David, Derrick's attorney. We discussed the original ask of me regarding Derrick's child. I was due to give my decision by the end of the week, but I was ready now. I had considered everything. I heard Derrick's thoughts. I had prayed on it. I had thought long and hard about this, and I have an answer, which is why I had called this meeting. I drove into downtown Kalamazoo. I parked my car in the parking lot adjacent to the tall building off of Michigan Ave. I walked into the lobby. I checked myself in the mirror as I pushed the elevator button to take me up. I don't know why I was so nervous. I held many meetings, done countless presentations, and closed deals like I was on a game show. This meeting would be no different.

The bell from the elevator signaled my arrival on the seventh floor that David's office occupied. I walked through the glass doors and was immediately greeted by the receptionist.

"Mrs. Montgomery, welcome back. David will be with you shortly. Can I get you something to drink?" she politely asked.

'Yeah, some whiskey," I replied under my breathe.

"Excuse me, I'm sorry I didn't hear you Mrs. Montgomery," she spoke.

"No, nothing, thank you" I quickly spoke up.

The last thing I need is a drink. I took a seat and waited for David to emerge. After waiting patiently for about ten minutes, David entered the reception area.

"Tracy, I'm so glad to see you" he spoke through his masked face.

"Hello, David, thank you for seeing me today" I replied, and I walked toward him.

He led the way down the hallway of neatly lined offices. We reached the end of the hallway and entered David's corner office. It was just as I remembered it being a few months back, except this time, I could hear the chitter chatter of a small voice and the crashing of toy cars. I turned my head to the left, and there in the corner was a small child. I looked at David as if to ask with my eyes, was that him? He shook his head, yes. I was in shock. There I was, standing inches away from the thing that had cursed my life, and I had come to hate so much. But in that instant, all I felt was joy like never before. Pure joy.

I removed my mask and walked toward the sounds. His eyes caught me watching him. He paused and stood up.

"Hi" the little voice said.

"Hi" I replied, holding back tears. "I'm Tracy" I continued.

"I know, are you my new mommy?" He asked with a puzzled look on his face.

"New mommy? What makes you ask that question?" I responded.

"My other mother died. She told me that my new mommy would come for me soon. She said her name would be Tracy, and she would love me and take good care of me. Are you her?" His big, beautiful eyes filled with hope asked me again.

I looked back at David. I smiled

"I sure am," I said to my surprise.

He rushed into my legs, holding me so tight. With one car in his hand. He held me like I was his wish granted by Santa. The tears rolled down my face as I laughed and hugged him back. I bent down and hugged him tight as we both shared tears of joy.

"What took you so long?" He asked.

"I don't know, but I'm here now baby. I'll never be late again." I confidently said.

I could feel my heart beating fast. Matthew Montgomery had taken a piece of my heart that had been closed off in a matter of seconds. He had opened his heart to me, and who was I to deny him access to mines. He broke his grip on me only to retrieve his jacket and other toy car. He rushed back by my side. We sat at David's desk. I had finalized the custody paperwork and my signature was notarized. I asked if Matthew had anything else with him. David said no; unfortunately, he did not have much.

"No worries, we can fix that" I said, smiling at Matthew. He smiled back and that's when I noticed those dimples. I had seen them only on Derrick. It was the best part of making Derrick laugh. It was everything seeing them again. "You look just like your daddy" I proudly confessed to Matthew.

"I do?" He asked.

"Yes, you do, and I'll tell you all about him if you would like" I stated as the tears rolled down my face.

Matthew took his free hand and wiped my tears off my face. "Don't cry, I'm here now." The brave little boy spoke.

"Yes, you are. Yes, you are," I cried, hugging him tight as David watched.

Matthew put on his jacket, grabbed my hand, and waved goodbye to David. Together we walked side by side out the office, onto the elevator, and into the unknown. Oh, I wish Derrick could see this. I hope he knew how much he was right. I needed Matthew and he needed me. It wasn't my intention. I wanted to say no. I went up there to sign him over to the state. But all I saw was Derrick. All I saw was the brother of Jackson, and I thought how selfish of me not to want him. How disappointed Jackson would be in his mother. I thought about my unborn son I was carrying, growing up without his brothers. I thought about Derrick wanting all of us to be together. I wanted him to be wrong, but he always knew what was best for me. He knew me better than anyone. Today was no exception. I hope he knows how much I love him right now. I hope this made his heart rejoice because it sure did mines.

"Matthew" I spoke softly,

"Yes, Mommy" he spoke without hesitation.

"What do we do now?" I asked.

"Can we go home?" he asked, looking up into my eyes.

"Home it is Matthew. Let's go home" I stated.

The Past

I was smiling again. Not just on the exterior but also internally. Work was going well. Derrick was finally stable. Even when he had moments of depression, it was nothing like what had transpired in the past. We were moving forward. We were finally at a place where my faith in the health care system was restored and the institution of marriage had me seeing things with rose colored glasses.

Derrick's mother came to visit us shortly after his father passed away. It was hard on Derrick and his mom. I thought it would be best if she came and spent some time with us. This way, Derrick wouldn't be alone in his grieving and neither would his mom. I wasn't sure either one of them should be alone right now. Derrick was managing better than I had expected. He had increased his therapy sessions to twice a week, at the news of his father's passing. It showed he was maturing in managing his mental health. Derrick's mother on the other hand, was not faring well at all. She brought all the baggage she could carry from their marriage to our home and unleashed a garbage bag of secrets and skeleton bones on Derrick who was ill prepared to deal with her and her drama.

Through my research and in dealing with Derrick, I had come to notice the common straits of those dealing with mental illness. I did not have a degree or anything, just things I had noticed, committed to memory, observed, and thought I was wiser because I was living in it with someone going through it. The lies, the tricks, the games they played. I thought I was as prepared as I could be for Derrick's next episode. But It wasn't Derrick I had to worry about. It was Ms. Rebecca's antics that I should have sharpened my skills on.

It all started when she came to visit us. At first, everyone seemed to be handling the Death of Mr. Montgomery as best they could. Rebecca and Derrick would share stories of their dearly beloved. They would laugh at times gone and recall some of his favorite sayings, books, and songs. Derrick danced with his mom as he held her and reminded her how much his father cared for her. It seemed to bring both of them comfort. It wasn't until Rebecca started mixing the reminiscing with alcohol that the nightly routine became a daily haul. She would wake up smelling like last night. She would try to disguise her pain with perfume's smell, which cheapened her most expensive bottle. At first, I let it go. But when the pattern emerged, I told Derrick about my concerns. That did not go over so well.

I had underestimated the bond between a mother and her son. Rebecca knew it too. She played on Derrick's love for her. One casual drink became several, and then a daily ritual. I had warned Derrick of over drinking with his medicine and the effects of his behaviors. But for every word of affirmation and accountability I provided to Derrick, his mom countered. I got rid of all the alcohol, and she would buy more. Pretty soon, Derrick and Rebecca had hiding spots around the house. She encouraged him to miss his therapy sessions because she needed him. Rebecca conveniently always needed somewhere to be around the same time Derrick needed to be at therapy. I would offer to take her, but she insisted she spends quality time with her son. Derrick obliged like a good son, to the detriment of his well-being.

I was losing the battle. Not only was Derrick missing his therapy sessions, but there were days where he forgot to take his medicine. There were days I noticed that he still had medicine in his weekly medication slots. My friendly reminders became annoyances to him and his mother. I was an outsider in my own home. Derrick's behavior started to resemble the demon we had fought so hard to escape. His mother was a whole other demon. I had refused to entertain either one of them.

I would work longer hours and eat before heading home, just to avoid the alcohol-stained conversations. Derrick started to resent me for my absence or unwillingness to participate. On more than one occasion, I was told I prevented him from having fun that I made him sick. Or the insult that stung the hardest, why did I marry someone like you. I tried to ignore his rants, but truth be told, it hurt. His words made it obvious that he did not appreciate the sacrifices I had made for him, the pain and tears his behavior had caused. The permanent scars that stretched across my body reminded me of the loss we shared. His words were soaked in blood, and the laughter from his mother's echoes in agreeance cosigned the torment I was under.

I had decided to leave. I had packed my bags. I decided to rent an apartment in secret. I was done. I had nothing more to give. And as much as I wanted to make my marriage work, I was fighting a battle with no armor or weapons. Even when I thought I was prepared, I wasn't ready. The back and forth of Derrick, giving into his mental illness hindered my growth and mental well-being. I was losing my sanity. I had to go. It was the only way I was going to find my peace. That was more important than saving Derrick and even throwing a life jacket at Rebecca. Just when I was done, he pulled me back in.

I had received a call on my cell phone while at work. The number called back several times in a row. I had ignored it at first. I was in a meeting facilitating a presentation. By the time the meeting was over, there were 15 missed calls and 4 messages. I walked back to my office, closed the door, and pressed play.

"Mrs. Montgomery, this is Bronson Hospital. Your Husband and his mother were in a serious car crash. If you can give us a call back as soon as you get this message...." the concerned voice uttered.

I immediately called the number back and Identified myself. The shock of what she was telling me. I had forgotten how mad I was at Derrick and his mother. All I knew was I had to get there. I had to get to him. Just then, I looked up and could see two officers walking my way. The receptionist was escorting them from the lobby. She knocked on my door. By the look on my face, they knew that I had been informed of the accident. They were there to escort me to the hospital safely. In all the commotion, I had forgotten that I was trying to escape the madness of the Montgomery name and instantly became another pawn in the Montgomery game of life.

The Present

~

The sounds of Matthew playing around the house or the pitter patter of his feet shuffling from room to room brought instant joy to my heart. It was the air that I was missing. Every day seemed brighter now that he and I were together. Who would have ever thought that I needed this? Matthew's creation had been the wedge in Derrick and my marriage. It was the topic of endless arguments and countless sleepless nights. It marked the beginning of what I had referred to as the end of us. Now, as I look back, it was the source of love. The act of unsolicited betrayal between a stranger and a hollowed mind was now the center of my world, a gift left behind for me to unwrap and cherish.

Over the next few days, Matthew and I became acquainted. I learned which cereals he preferred. That he enjoyed watching cartoons and science shows. His favorite color was blue and just like Derrick, apple juice was his drink of choice for breakfast. There were other similarities that were shared between Derrick and Matthew. The way they walked, the way they held their heads, and yes, those dimples. It was so weird how two people who had never met had so much in common. For Matthew, it was all new. He said the house was so big, he had his own room, he loved his new books, and he clung close to me no matter what we did. My new shadow had latched on, and we were inseparable.

We had decorated his room to his taste. What we couldn't find at some of the area stores, we ordered online. Every day was like Christmas as boxes arrived for Matthew. The excitement in his eyes and the smile on his face made answering the door worthwhile. Watching him tear open the boxes and announce the contents made me laugh. He would then grab my hand and up the stairs, we would go. He would show me where to place items and would clap when we completed our task. At night I would tuck him into his big boy bed as he referred to it, read him a story, and kiss him on the forehead. But that wouldn't last. As soon as I would get comfortable in my bed, I would hear his little feet at my bedroom door. He would wait for me to answer and come running in.

I shared with Matthew that I was expecting a little brother for him. He was so glad. He would rub his baby brother every chance he got. To practice his reading, he would make me have a seat so that he could read to my tummy. It was everything that I would have wanted Jackson to be able to participate in. Not that I wished Jackson were Matthew. It was times like this that I wished things had turned out differently for my son. But then I don't think my heart would have been open to loving Matthew. At this moment, right here, I could love them all perfectly, each in their own way. Matthew made it easy to love. Just the sound of him calling me mommy seemed like second nature. With open arms, he accepted me, my flaws and all. It was the love of a child that had tamed me. Matthew's kindness made me look at my behavior over the past few months and question if I was the person I had presented to the world. He made me want to be better. For him, my unborn child, for Jackson's memory, and Derrick. Most importantly, his love made me whole, offered a puzzle piece to my soul that had been missing. It was the calm that gave me my sanity back.

I finally got around to Derrick's next letter. With all of Matthew's commotion and creating a place for him, I had focused my energy on him. I had hoped that Derrick was pleased with my decision. I think somewhere deep down, and he knew that I would make this choice. That he didn't even have to ask me, but he did. And as I look at Matthew's face as he lay sound asleep on the pillow next to me, I'm glad that I did. I opened the envelope and began to read the letter.

My Sweet Red,

If I didn't tell you this enough, I am so proud of the woman you are. You have always been a pillar of strength and wise beyond your years. You held a career, our home and me down. Even when you thought I wasn't watching you move, I was. I had studied you as if you were a college course I needed to graduate with honors. You are complicated, stubborn, loveable, creative and relentless. You gave me courage in moments of darkness and brought me joy in times of sorrow. And yet, with everything that has happened, you're holding your head up high and pushing forward. I pray that you are doing it with a smile on your face.

I also hope that you remember more of the good times we shared, and in time all the painful memories fade into the night. Especially now that you have company. I pray that you made the best decision for you, and that your heart had room for both Matthew and our son. Knowing what I know now, I wished that all three of my sons would have known the love of you, their mother. What a privilege it is to know that you are caring for them. I can't even imagine the fun, laughter and things that you all will get into. I laugh at the thought of the memories you will create with them and my heart becomes full.

You are one special woman. And that is why this next request, I'm relieved to know that I am not asking you in person for fear of what you would throw at me or the backlash of words that may spew out at me. Keep in mind that if I could, I would've and should've repaired the relationship between you and my mother. I was the prize my mother refused to share. Even when I knew that her attachment was unhealthy, I allowed her to hold on to me. I think as I look back, Rebecca was my enabler. In no way am I excusing my behavior. I accept that my mental health has brought us to this place we are at right now. But Rebecca allowed me to stay low in my depression, she allowed me to entertain the thoughts in my mind. It was the complete opposite of what you requested of me. When I didn't want to be held accountable for my demons, Rebecca looked the other way. I loved her and cursed her for it. I hated that she provided a way out that was easier than the direction you needed me to run in.

That is why this ask is so important. Because I know you've disliked Rebecca, I know that you are twisting up your lips while reading these words. It's time Tracy. It's time for you and her to mend your relationship. You have to for the boys. You're going to need the help. And with no other family to offer support, allow Rebecca an opportunity to right her wrongs. It can be different. It will be. This time the roles have been reversed. You're the mom now, and she will have to play by your rules if she wants an opportunity to be a part of our sons' lives. I know you won't allow her to do to them what she did to me. But first, you'll have to take a leap of faith and let her back in. You'll need to forgive her. You'll need to love her again, just like you learned to love and forgive me.

Tracy, there is another reason you may want to forgive Rebecca. Forgive her for you. Rebecca represents everything that is wrong with a family dealing with mental illness. She kept her mental health a secret, she kept mines a secret, and even when I was falling apart, she still denied it. I know you blame her for many issues we had in our marriage almost as much as you blame me, which is why you need to let it go. No more anger. No more unhealthy energy, no more holding onto secrets and feelings. I need you to be free of all of it. Free to take care of the boys and yourself without feeling any remorse or guilt. Can you do that, Tracy? Can you do that for me? Can you do it for yourself?

Open your heart one last time for me and help me mend the strained relationship with my mom. Something tells me that she needs this just as much as you. I don't really know how you should go about doing this, but Matthew and our unborn son would be one helluva reason to get her to come visit if I had to guess. It would also give you an opportunity to show me again just how loving, patient and, smart you are.

Don't look like that. Yes, I know the face you're making right now. It makes your forehead wrinkle. You are too cute for that. I love you Tracy, and if anyone can pull this off, it would be you.

Good night Sweet Red, I love you always.

Derrick

The Past

The battle between mothers and wives for the coveted first place position in the male child's heart is as old as time. It is a vicious cycle that has been repeated over and over again, causing arguments, sleepless nights, and divorce. In my case, the reward was death.

At first, Rebecca and I were the best of friends. She eagerly awaited my visits. The shopping sprees, lunch dates, and candid conversations lead me to believe that I was welcomed into their family. Even though Derrick had not popped the question, according to the Montgomery's, I was as close to a daughter that they were going to get, without birthing me themselves. There was always talk of Derrick and I getting married. Rebecca was the first to initiate the conversation. I would just play along and sometimes allow myself to become lost in the dream. Mr. Montgomery would remind Derrick of what a catch I was and when he would make an honest woman out of me. Derrick and I would just smile and shake our heads.

So, it was no surprise when Derrick actually asked me for my hand in marriage. Everyone was so excited. Derrick had it all planned out so perfectly. It was following my graduation. Derrick's parents and my mom all made the trip to Kalamazoo for the big day. I was told no one else was able to attend the ceremony. I recall walking off the stage and being met with the cheers of excited parents, balloons, and flowers. In the middle of it all was Derrick. I remember feeling like the world was perfect. I was surrounded by people who loved me and genuinely cared for me.

Derrick had planned a dinner celebration right after the ceremony. I had just enough time for a few photo ops with friends and family. He quickly whisked us off to one of our favorite spots, downtown Kalamazoo. It was literally five minutes away from our current location. I could not understand his rushed behavior. But with all the excitement of the day, it didn't matter. I was finally a graduate with a bachelor's degree. We parked our cars in the parking ramp and made the walk across the street and into Rustica. The waitress greeted us promptly, and we were seated right away. I sat with my back toward the door, which I came to understand was by design. Our table was located in the center of the restaurant. This was odd because normally, Derrick preferred the cozier locations that lined the wall of the restaurant. I reasoned that it was because we were part of a bigger crowd we sat where we could.

Our server made his way through the crowded restaurant and over to our table. Derrick ordered two bottles of champagne and I added water with lemon to the list. The server nodded his head, and off he went to place our drink request. While waiting, the conversation at the table turned slightly as Derrick began to speak. Now Derrick was usually very conservative in public places. He used his inside private voice so that our conversations stayed with us. But his voice today carried across the room. I shot him a look to signal him to lower his voice, but he just smiled at me flashing his dimples. He continued speaking and soon had the full attention of everyone in the restaurant.

To my surprise, I started closely examining the faces of those in the restaurant. The smiles from onlookers soon were replaced with familiar faces of family, friends, coworkers, and my sorority sisters. That's when Derrick's words and actions started to make sense. He grabbed my hand and pulled me out of my seat. He spoke words of affirmation and truth about his feelings for me. He told stories of the first time we meet and how he prayed I would not take D' Markus back. That he searched for me on campus for two months before that fateful day when he called my name, I answered and agreed to have lunch with him. How from that day, we had been inseparable. How he could not imagine having me in his life. How he wanted to spend forever making me happy and how he would be honored if I would be his wife. That's when it happened. I stood in front of a room of those that loved us both, watch Derrick bow as if being knighted by royalty, he began to speak the words I had hoped one day to hear.

"Tracy Marie Scott, I love you more than you will ever know. You are the light that makes my day bright, the calm that compliments my peace. You are the air in my atmosphere and the gravity that keeps me grounded. You bring purpose to all my plans, and your smile makes my heart rejoice. I would be eternally honored if you would be my wife and share your world with me. Will you marry me? Derrick confidently spoke while looking me in my eyes.

Without hesitation, I shook my head and whispered yes, yes and yes over and over again.

"Say it louder!" someone shouted.

"Yes, Derrick, Yes!" I screamed out loud as tears of joy flowed down my face. "Yes!" I repeated as he stood up to wipe the tears away by kissing me gently where each tear had fallen. He held me in his arms as the room full of loved ones cheered in excitement and approval. I just recall wanting that feeling never to end. Derrick and I were as perfect for each other in every way and now the world knew it too.

Now one would have thought that my future mother-in-law would have been elated by the news. After all, she spent years engaging in conversations and talks about Derrick and I marrying. But shortly after the proposal, Rebecca's true colors started to show. Her sly remarks about my curvy frame became a concern for her. She made insulting comments about my choices in dresses. She tried forcing her style on me by insisting that I try on dresses she chose during my dress fittings. My mother had asked me to just play along and reminded me that trying on dresses was supposed to be fun.

"Ultimately, it's your decision, and I'll make sure that everyone knows that." My mom whispered in my ear as she smiled at me, giving me the confidence to just brave the day's activities.

But that wasn't the last of Rebecca's antics. It seemed that nothing I did or said was good enough for Derrick, our wedding, or her. She had the nerve to call the catering company and change the menus for the reception. By the time I had found out, it was too late to make any changes, so I was forced to comply with her changes. I tried to communicate my concerns with Derrick, but he wanted nothing to do with it. He would just suggest that I try to get both mothers more engaged in the planning process so that no one felt left out. However, my mom was not the problem, it was his mother who was becoming the thorn in my side.

It didn't stop there. We made it through the wedding. To our surprise, his mother and father joined us on our honeymoon. His father had no idea that the vacation Rebecca had planned impeded our time alone. In fact, no one knew where we were going. Later Derrick told me he had mentioned it to his mother for emergency purposes. He had no clue that she would use that information as an opportunity to infringe on our honeymoon. I moved past that situation. When Derrick and I purchased our new home, she insisted on coming house shopping with us. She traveled every chance she could to join us. She wanted to gift us the money for the house, but I felt that she would assume she had a say over where I laid my head at night by accepting the money. Luckily, Derrick and I saw eye to eye on accepting her generous gift.

It was a continuous cycle of her overpowering behavior, and her need to be between Derrick and I, and the unhealthy way she went about catering to him as if he was still a child. I attempted to approach Rebecca, woman to woman and have an adult conversation. Needless to say, that did not go over well. Her once loving words became hurtful and mean. It was at that point that I knew I would never win her over. I also knew that unless Derrick put his foot down and take my side, chose me over his mother, that her behavior would continue as is. So, I stopped trying. Rebecca became Mrs. Montgomery once again. I kept the conversations a polite formality and, her visits a diplomatic chore.

The worse confrontation between Rebecca and I didn't happen until I lost Jackson. I was already at my lowest point in my marriage. Her visit wasn't welcome. Nor were her accusatory stares. One day when Derrick was at work, picking up a few files he needed while working from home, Rebecca took advantage of the time she had alone with me to express herself. His words stung like sharp knives piercing my soul. I had already played that night over and over again in my head. I had already played the would've, should've game and yet my son was still not here. I did not need her two cents of no value. The conversation soon changed into a shouting match and before I knew it, she had raised her hand and slapped me. What happened next, I wish I regretted it, it was not my intention to ever do what I did. It all happened so fast. She had followed me up the stairs. She could not stomach the things I had disclosed about her precious Derrick, right before she slapped me.

"Here, let me show you how that felt. How it felt to be scared out of your mind, scared that the stranger that had been your husband made me feel that night!" I screamed at her as I pushed her.

Her body fell backward and in slow motion, I watched as she fell down the same stairs my pregnant body had traveled. This time it was Rebecca. With every forced breath that escaped her body, I felt the pain all over again of that night. I couldn't recall every detail, but I knew. I knew that that fall was the reason Jackson was not with me. I watched as she landed at the bottom of the staircase. Her old body had taken an unexpected blow. She looked up at me and attempted to get up. Just then, I heard the door open. Derrick came rushing in to assist her. Rebecca sat there moaning, looking up at the empty staircase. I heard Derrick ask what happened. The only thing Rebecca said was he lost her balance and fell. Derrick looked up the stairs, I was no longer standing there. I had allowed the prince to rush in and save the day. Something that he had failed to do for me when she pushed and pushed and pushed at me. Finally, Rebecca knew what that felt like. All of it.

The Present

I tried ignoring Derrick's request. There was no way I wanted anything to do with Rebecca. I often wonder would Derrick be here if she had acknowledged the help her son needed when she had an opportunity to influence him. Her controlling and complicit ways contributed to Derrick's downfall. She aided in the demise of my marriage. She just wasn't the energy I wanted around me or my children.

A few days had passed since reading Derrick's letter. Matthew and I had attended doctors' appointments. He had a well child checkup, and I had an OBGYN follow up. It was Matthew's first time accompanying me to see the doctor. He was so excited. When I told him what we were doing today, he kept talking about seeing his new baby brudda. He even made up a song that he sang the entire car ride to both of our appointments. When we finally arrived at my doctor's appointment, Matthew announced to everyone that he was here to see inside his mommy's tummy and see his brudda. Everyone laughed. He was just a pleasure to be around. With his bright outlook on life, even with everything he had been through, he smiled. It was contagious.

Soon, Matthew and I were called back to the doctor's office. He jumped up grabbed my hand and hurried me through the open doors. We followed Melanie the nurse to our destination. I sat on the examination table and Matthew opted for the swivel chair that was usually reserved for the doctor. Within minutes Dr. Yvonne Smith had entered the room. She was the OBGYN that my primary doctor referred me to. She smiled at Matthew as she introduced herself to him, and like a little gentleman, he shook her hand and told her his name. Matthew exited his seat, then he came and stood next to me. He was holding my hand as if he was shy. She asked her normal questions and I replied. She took her measurements of my stomach as Matthew watched cautiously. She listened to my heartbeat and took a few other observations before Matthew lost his patience.

"When are you going to show me my baby Brudda?" He asked.

"Is that what you came here today for? Dr. Smith Asked.

Matthew shook his head as if to say yes.

"Well, let me get to it" Dr. Smith added as she winked at Matthew, making him blush.

Dr. Smith grabbed her ultrasound chart, while I pulled up my top and rolled down my pants to the bottom of my hips. Matthew held my hand tight. I could tell he was nervous and excited. There was a squirt of warm gel that was rubbed on my protruding belly. Matthew looked on. Dr. Smith took the wand and guided it across my abdomen. Within seconds, the image was on the screen. Matthew watched the monitor as if it were his favorite cartoon playing. And there he was, nestled inside me.

"Look Matthew!" I said, pointing at the screen.

With eyes wide open, Matthew said, "I SEE HIM, I SEE HIM MOMMY!" he screamed with excitement.

I smiled at the joy this brought Matthew. Dr. Smith smiled also. She continued to take her measurements of my growing baby. She monitored the steady beat of his heart as Matthew studied her every move.

"Is that his heartbeat?" He asked.

"Yes, it is" I confirmed.

"When will he be ready to come out?" Matthew quizzed.

"We have a few more months before he will be ready to come out," Dr. Smith jokingly stated. "Would you like a picture of your baby brother?" She asked Matthew.

"Yes, Please" He said as his eyes opened wide.

While Dr. Smith was printing off pictures for Matthew of his unborn brother, I wiped the gel off my stomach, freshened up, fixed my clothing, and waited for Dr. Smith to finish entertaining Matthew.

I was nearing my 30 weeks. As I look back, so much had happened in my world. In less than two months, I would bring a new child into this world alone. I was scared and frightened. I hadn't thought about who would care for Matthew for me when that time arrives. I hadn't thought passed today. I didn't know who would be in the room with me. I guess I had always assumed that it would have been Derrick. And now that he could not be here with me, I guess I hadn't realized just how alone I was. With both of my parents passing, it wasn't like I could call my mom up and fill her in on all the crazy shit that had happened in my life since the last time we spoke. My Dad passed away in my junior year at college. He had lost a long hard battle with cancer. Sure, I had cousins, aunties and uncles, but no one ever really takes the place of your mom and dad. And with everything that has happen, I really could have used their wisdom and guidance right now. I would settle for a hug or kiss from either one of them, especially now.

It was in that moment that I began to her Derricks words. They were clear. I understood why he asked what he did. As much as I hated him for putting me in this predicament, I loved the way he thought ahead. I just wished he could have imagined himself here with me. I was going to need help. I was going to need Rebecca, whether I wanted to accept it or not. I questioned how long it would be before I swallowed all my pride and asked her for help. It should be a cold day in hell before I do, but I've already been through hell and back. So I guess the question was, would I be willing to forgive Rebecca and allow her an opportunity to be a better grandmother than she was a mother?

It was Friday night. I had just tucked Matthew into bed. I was cuddled up in the bed under the covers. I reached for Derrick's letters just as my cellphone rang. I looked over at it and to my surprise, it was Rebecca. With everything that I had going on this week, it had slipped my mind to call her. I must have thought too much about her who shall not be named, and look here she was—calling at this less considerate time. I hesitated. I looked at the phone as it rang for the fifth time and without thinking, I answered.

"Hello, Tracy, it's Rebecca" She started the conversation.

"What can I do for you Rebecca?" I asked, cutting straight to the point.

"I know that it is late, I just had to call you." Rebecca spoke.

"What is so important that it couldn't wait until the morning? Is everything ok?" I questioned sternly.

"I... I..." Rebecca struggled to find the words.

"You what Rebecca? Are you sure you're ok?" I questioned further.

"Tracy. I received a letter from Derrick." She whispered.

There was a long pause.

"A letter?" I replied as my tone softened.

"Oh Tracy, I'm so sorry. I'm so sorry for everything. I was a poor excuse for a mother-in-law. I treated you like... I'm so ashamed. I'm so ashamed." She repeated as her voice cracked. I could tell that she was crying and trying to hold it together. There was another awkward pause.

"Derrick's letter. He told me... how horrible of a person I had been. Just how much pain I actually caused you, your marriage, and him. I thought..., I thought I was helping. I mean, I thought I was protecting him. I just didn't want him to suffer. I mean, I didn't want his illness to be a crutch for him, a label. I just wanted to protect him..." She cried.

I wanted to say something, but there were no words. Derrick must have sent a letter much like the ones he had left behind for me. If Rebecca's letter was anything like mines, Derrick did not hold back but finally used his letters to speak his truth and peace. I just never thought that he would be able to express himself to his mother. I guess I didn't even know he felt some kind of way about her behavior. I mean, I had tried countless times to bring it to his attention with no acknowledgement from him. I don't think he ever mentioned anything to her that I brought to his attention. So, all of this was a surprise to me.

"I was wondering if I could come to visit with you for a while so that we could talk face to face." Rebecca pleaded.

To her surprise, I responded quickly to her request. "Rebecca, I would love for you to come visit. Besides, I have a few surprises for you. I've been meaning to reach out to you too. But yes, you should come." I calmly and mildly reaffirmed.

"This is great! I will make plans to join you soon. I can't wait to see what surprises you have for me." Rebecca cheered up and spoke.

I smiled. I smiled harder at the surprises that awaited her arrival. Rebecca had no idea what was in store for her. I hoped that she meant every word of her apology because this visit would prove once and for all if she was worthy of this second chance she has been given, not only with Matthew, but with our unborn child.

"That sounds great Rebecca" I concluded my part of the conversation.

"Tracy..." She spoke. There was another pause. "Thank you for picking up the phone. I don't think I would have if I were you." She commented.

"Good night Rebecca" I lovingly added.

"Good Night Tracy, my dear, Good Night" Rebecca replied.

It looks like Derrick had a plan just in case I hadn't come to my senses. And maybe it was best Rebecca approached me first. Somehow the apology sounded a little more authentic with her making the first move. Maybe Derrick knew that was how it needed to be from the start. Maybe his letter to me wasn't about me making the first move to reconcile Rebecca and my relationship, but more so of me being open to receiving the apology from her. I hated when Derrick was right. I hated it even more that he wouldn't be here to witness this truce.

The Past

By the time my mother passed, Derrick's mental health had deteriorated. He had refused any help. He wasn't taking the medication prescribed by his now fourth doctor and going to therapy sessions was out of the question. I had hidden in the shadows of despair, wondering if saving him was worth the heartache and pain. If losing myself was worth the fight. The only other person I've talked about Derrick to was my mother. She was my best friend, especially as I aged and matured. She gave me encouragement, wisdom, and insight that I struggled to maintain during one of his many episodes. Her words would echo in my mind every time I wanted to leave. Every time I tried to run away, escape the madness that had become the acceptable trauma of normal in the Montgomery household. I wanted out. But my love for Derrick, his hold on me, the history, kept pulling me back. Lord knows I tried, but I always ended up right where I began, in the secluded cul de sac that masked the imperfections I lived.

I remember trying to confide in a few friends. I desperately wanted to scream at the top of my lungs what I was going through. But every time I tried, people dismissed what I was trying to say even before I could tell the story.

"Girl, Derrick is the best thing for you," "I'm sure whatever the issue is you and Derrick can work through it," "Not you two, the perfect couple has issues? No way", or my favorite "Girl be happy you have a man that loves you". I had heard them all. So, I stopped trying. I just held it all in. I kept every guarded episode, every argument, every tear to myself. I had hardened my heart like a diamond pressed back into coal. It became difficult for me to see past the obvious damage that had been done. Not just to myself and my marriage but also to Derrick. Now, I think that once I gave up, he gave in too. We both stopped fighting. Although I never said it out loud, he knew. I'm sure he saw it on my face. I wore it like the makeup that enhanced my beauty. Only it became a permeant beauty mark that wouldn't fade away.

His mother, my mother, his dad and mines had led me to believe that I was wrong in my behavior and actions. I guess they were going to set me straight. Show me that marriage's commitment was deeper than the good days and lived in the dark lonely moments, when you wanted to give in. Well, I was past that. The hell I was living couldn't be consoled by any of their words. So, the lies, the secrets, the fear, the solitude, and loneliness crept in. It was there that I found comfort. I had come to know this place all too well, and I survived there. I smiled when needed, I laughed void of feeling, and lived in a state of acceptance of my ignorance, his ignorance, my selfishness, his selfishness, and our untenanted shell of a marriage.

The Present

My sessions with Dr. Mary had become easier. I was lifting the veil and lowering the walls I had built up around me. I had begun to see the consequences of my behavior and how it affected both Derrick and me. The things you don't understand are often the hardest to grasp. I had no idea how to support Derrick in his journey. I now know that my words carried merit, maybe too much value, especially when I used them in battle with Derrick. I knew they hurt, hell I was often unapologetic about them. I know now how that could have factored into his behavior.

Dr. Mary's guidance allowed me to see past myself and my pain and look at the marriage. There were certain things that I could have done differently. There were times I should have pulled closer than push away. I should have done many things differently had I known what I know now. The issue is I can't. I can't undo the years of pain and heartache. I can't take back my words. I can't un anything that happens between Derrick and me. What I had learned and will try to do every day moving forward is forgive. I will forgive him. I now know not just through these sessions but from hearing Derrick's own words that he was worth it. He loved me the best way he could. It was me who couldn't see it. His mental illness was a master manipulator. It knew he loved me and I him, and saw to it that it kept us apart. That was its strength. Apart we both were vulnerable to its tactics; we could not win a game with no rules. But together, we could have. We could have fought together. We could have supported each other.

We could have built up a wall and allowed faith and God to reign. It was part of our vows that we had missed. That I had missed. We said our vows in fort of God and a host of witnesses. We... I had forgotten that and excluded God from the equation. Now don't get me wrong, I couldn't pray Derrick's illness away, but I could have asked for protection for him, that God give him the strength to battle on and fight through his illness. Instead, I turned a blind eye and walked in the opposite direction.

It's funny the things you see so clearly once the veil has been lifted and you allow the light in. The storm had passed, and I was still living under the clouds. I smiled, knowing that Derrick was watching and knew that I had finally lifted my head high once again. That when I laughed now, it was full of life and love. It was funny too that all my memories of him now were good memories even when the circumstances might be blurred, the focus was on him and not the illness. I could distinguish the difference now. Everything was clearer, not without blemish, just clearer and I liked what I was seeing.

I had let Dr. Mary in on the upcoming visit with Rebecca. I shared my feelings and concerns. As always, she never gave her personal opinion, but allowed me to self-discover my next steps. I knew what I needed to do. I also shared how Matthew and I were getting along. So far, this had been the best thing for me. Matthew was perfect. In so many ways, he was Derrick. I had imagined he and Jackson would have been best friends. I also knew that if Jackson were here, I probably would not have made room for Matthew in my heart. Matthew made me smile. I have to give his mother some credit. I had hated her for years. I didn't know her, just what I thought she represented. But she had done a great job with Matthew. Especially in preparing Matthew for me. He came with open arms and a heart just as big. He made loving again so easy.

Dr. Mary commented on my progress. I was even impressed by the journey I had taken. From the first time I walked through her office doors until today, I almost forgot what my version was like. I had cried for her. I was so happy that she took the steps to get us here. I had to thank her for all she had endured. I wanted her to know we were doing fine, that everything was going to be ok. My appointments had adjusted from several a week, to weekly, bi-weekly, and now to monthly conversations. Yes, I was making progress, and it showed. Not just in my appearance, but in my heart and soul. I had been freed and finally could own the person I was. The good, bad, and the ugly.

The Present

I had the car service pick Rebecca up from the airport. I had informed her that I did not want to keep her waiting because of my tight schedule. I would make sure I was home by the time she was set to arrive. I know she was a little disappointed in my unconventional greeting, but I didn't want to spoil the surprises that I had in store for her. After all, if we were going to have a fresh start, I wanted it to be on my terms and where I was comfortable. It took me a long time to feel this way and just in case it did not go as planned, at least I was in the confines of my own home.

I heard the town car pull up in the circular round-about that outlined the entrance to the house. I heard the car door open and the chatter of two people talking. I peeked out the window and could see Rebecca masked up and escorting the slender built man who was carrying her luggage to the door. The doorbell rang as I took a deep breath and smiled and opened the door. Rebecca seemed shocked. Even through the mask, I could tell she wasn't expecting me to be in such a cordial manner. I thanked the gentleman for his assistance and tipped him accordingly as I welcomed Rebecca into the house.

It wasn't her first visit, but her actions seemed to suggest she was a little hesitant. And why wouldn't she be? We shared our last moments here just months earlier had cast the biggest cloud over us and our relationship. I wasn't sure if I would ever speak to her again. Hell, I assumed that we had spoken all the ill-intentioned hurtful things two people could share. And yet, here we were, standing in silence like strangers. I smiled again at her as she lifted her eyes off the floor and finally took a good, hard look at me. A real hard look, past my face and stared at my whole body. Her eyes widened and I heard her gasp.

The silence was broken as tears of joy swept across Rebecca's face. She removed her mask and spoke.

"You're Pregnant?" she asked.

"Yes" I replied, smiling at her as I grabbed her hand and laid it on my protruding belly.

Rebecca laughed and cried simultaneously. "Oh, my goodness, oh, my Glory!" she exclaimed.

"Rebecca, there is more." I added

"More? What could be better than this?" she questioned.

I instructed her to have a seat. She looked puzzled by my request. But I rather she is sitting and not standing for the next surprise. I asked her to close her eyes and told her I would be right back.

I went and retrieved Matthew from his playroom. He was dressed like the perfect little gentleman. He wanted to look his best for his first meeting with his grandmother. In my conversations with Matthew, he had informed me that he did not know his real mothers' family. According to David, the attorney, there was no mention of any surviving relatives on Jessica's side of the family. So, I began sharing with Matthew all the wonderful grandparents, cousins, aunts and uncles that he would soon have the opportunity to meet. That he came from a slew of people who would love him unconditionally. That excited him. When I told him that his only surviving grandparent was coming to visit, he wanted to be perfect. He picked out his outfit like he was going for an interview. He had been practicing introducing himself to her all morning long. He even asked if we could get flowers for her, which we did after my morning appointments. Needless to say, Matthew was ready. Even when I wasn't, he showed me the way.

Matthew and I walked into the room. I instructed Rebecca to open her eyes. Matthew and I stood there in the center of the living room. Rebecca sat bewildered. The stunned look on her face mimicked mines when I first saw Matthew and his resemblance to Derrick. He walked up to her slowly. He looked back at me for reassurance. I shook my head as if to say go ahead. He extended his hand that was carrying the flowers he had picked for Rebecca and softly spoke.

"Hello, my name is Matthew Damon Montgomery. These are for you." Matthew proudly and nervously stated.

Rebecca took the flowers from Matthew's small hand. She just stared at him. No words, just stares. She would look over at me and then at Matthew, then do it over and over again.

"Matthew, sweetie, can you give us a moment?" I asked.

"Yes, mommy. Did I do good? Is she in shock, like we talked about?" Matthew tried to whisper but had failed at mastering his soft voice.

I watched as Matthew exited the room and headed back toward his playroom.

"How?" Rebecca questioned.

I went on to answer Rebecca's question. I went on to spin the same tale that had pained me for so many years. I told her how Derrick didn't want anyone to know about that night, how I had kept his secret, all of them. How we thought Jessica had gone through with the abortion and how I recently found out that she didn't. I shared with her the struggle to accept him, but I just knew he was meant for me to love when I saw him. I shared how Derrick knew that he was alive but didn't want to meet him. How he worried about the effects his mental illness would play on Matthew and our unborn child. He was fearful of repeating what had happened with Jackson that he wanted to protect them at all cost. That he may have taken his life for this reason and so many more.

Unlike any of my previous conversations with Rebecca, she did not interrupt me. She didn't cut her eyes, no twisting of her lips or any other exaggerated body language that showed her disapproval of me or the topic I engaged her in. She sat there, taking it all in. The tears rolled down her face. Maybe for the first time, she was open to hearing about Derrick and the challenges his mental illness had on him, the consequences of his actions, and possibly some of the reasons he may have taken his life. It was also the first time she heard the truth about our marriage. The parts that were not on display for the world to see. The pieces of Derrick that were reserved only for my eyes to witness. I had told it all. And for the first time outside of therapy, someone else knew also. Without hesitation, judgement, and fear of rejection, I had released my burdens and finally, breathed a clear sign of relief.

I finished a tale of two Derricks, the one Rebecca knew and loved and the Derrick that I had grown accustomed to loving. A story of a man loved and respected by all, and yet, couldn't allow himself to live in that love. Oh, the pain he must have been in, to miss out on this. This moment right here. Me carrying his child, me accepting Matthew as my own, and his mother, finally, willingly accepting him and all his imperfections. Rebecca felt it too. We sat in silence. Rebecca now had the full picture of Derrick and me. She, like so many, had only seen the play we performed. But the curtain was up. There was no makeup, pretty costumes, or scripts to follow. We were as raw and uncut as a manuscript could be in a rough draft. After a few minutes of Rebecca digesting our reality, she spoke.

"I had no idea. I'm so sorry, you poor girl, I didn't know" She cried.

"I know. Derrick... I mean I planned it that way. No one was supposed to know. I loved your son more than I loved myself at times. I just wanted to protect him. I just didn't understand how to. I just did not know if I could. And now, here we are. I guess we both now know" I attested as I comforted Rebecca.

"But... You... All this time, I thought you... I blamed you..." Rebecca cried.

"It's ok Rebecca. I blamed you, I blamed you too." I tried comforting Rebecca.

It was like a veil had been lifted. There was no screaming match, just two women that loved a man unconditionally. A wife and a mother coming to grips with the reality that they had been wrong. That they had placed blame on each other that was reserved for the misunderstanding of Derrick's mental illness. The lack of knowing and understanding it had placed on them the ignorance to see past that had caused so much pain and time to go by. Instead of being allies, they were sworn enemies. Together, who knows, but maybe, they could have been the force to penetrate through to Derrick, and possibly help him win the war he fought daily. What mattered was they were together now. A united force to move forward for the benefit of the Montgomery men in front of them now.

The Present

My Dearest Tracy,

I'm imagining that you and my mother know just how much in common you really have. I had always wanted her to love you like I do. I know that my illness complicated things between you and her. I wished that you had told her. Told her all about me and the issues with my mental illness. Maybe it would have helped. Not so much me, but it helped both of you to understand just how much you needed each other.

By now, I'm sure you've addressed the elephant in the room. My mother now knows all about my secrets. I did not mean to burden you with this task. I hoped that you would finally be freed of the secrets, the lies, and the hurt holding all that in for so many years has caused. By at least sharing that with my mother would allow her to see you for the caring and loving wife, you had always been to me. It would give Rebecca an opportunity to see firsthand who her son was, and that you were never the enemy. This also means that you've told her about Matthew, the circumstances surrounding him, what really happened that night we lost Jackson and shared the news about our unborn son. Hopefully, Matthew and our son can be the pride and joy she always wanted. Maybe they could be the right for all the wrong I've done. I pray that both of the boys are the best parts of me. And, that you and my mom can celebrate them together.

So, tell me how is it going? You and Matthew? You and the baby? My mother and you? There are so many things I want to be there to witness, but I won't be. My time is coming, and the pain gets heavier and harder to bear. I want you to know that I will always be there watching over you. That you now have the best parts of me with you. Whenever you look at the boys, my sons, you'll be reminded of all the good times we shared. All the positive qualities that lay deep within me. The attributes that I could not always show you, they can.

Take this time to make sure you live in these moments. You and I both know time will pass you by quickly. Look at how we started our relationship, at a chance interaction. You swept me off my feet from the first time I saw you. I knew then and I know now that you are the only woman for me. I just wish I had time on my side. Or better yet, time waited for me to get my mind right, slowed down just a little so that my thoughts were clear and my actions understandable. That I could make you see, make you understand just how much I love you. Besides, I need you to treasure the time you spend with our sons. The time will go by so fast. And with my mom's age and health, I'm not sure how much time you'll have her there to help before she too becomes a burden. Enjoy the time you have with them, do it for me. I wish I could be there. I wish I had time.

Tracy, I almost forgot to tell you thank you. You didn't have to do any of the requests I asked. I certainly do not deserve your kindness or love. I know that you've openly embraced Matthew, even when I couldn't. I know that you've made amends with my mother and that she is there assisting you. Even after all the drama, your heart is still so big and forgiving. Thank you for not changing. Thank you for being the filter of light and love in my life. Especially now that I am no longer there.

Tonight, I imagine that you are smiling. That you look radiant in your pregnancy glow and that for maybe the first time in a long time, I might have something to do with it. Keeping smiling Tracy, it looks good on you. Keep smiling baby, Keep smiling for me.

Love Always

Derrick,

I read Derrick's letter and smiled. He was right. It was like he knew me better than I knew myself. I did have a big heart, even when I did not want to admit it. I was full of forgiveness and even when I wanted to hold a grudge. Although there were things I chose to forgive, there were many things in my marriage that were unforgettable. I controlled the verse in which those events played out. I know that now. I also know what role I played in those events. I wasn't always the damsel in distress, sometimes I was just as wicked as the witch I wanted saving from.

It was also true that I needed Rebecca and Matthew in my life. I needed to create memories that would last more than the pain and hurt that had plagued me for so long. I needed reminders of just how lucky I had been to be Mrs. Derrick Allen Montgomery. Some things to outlive the negative images and thoughts I created in my mind. Memories that only Matthew and my unborn child could provide. I wanted to see the positivity that lay within Derrick. I needed the guidance of a mother to help me through this. I needed someone to join me on this journey, someone who knew the pain of losing a child and a husband. Someone who could remind me to stand tall and walk with pride. Rebecca offered that to me.

As far as how I was doing, only time would tell. And as Derrick reminded me, time waits for no one. It was past due that I learn to forgive freely and love openly, because before you know it, it would be too late.

I smiled, knowing he knew me all too well. I smiled because for the first time, I could clearly hear him. I could see him for who he really was. I smiled because he truly did make me happy. Even in death, he had made me smile.

The Past

I was so excited, the day I had planned for and awaited my entire life was finally here. I woke up knowing that my days' end, I would be Mrs. Derrick Allen Montgomery. Despite the past few months' complications, I was sure that marrying Derrick was the right thing to do. He had earned a place in my heart. I trusted that whatever was going on with him, I could offer the support and love he needed to either battle through it or manage it. I was prepared to offer that much of myself to him and this marriage. I knew it was far from perfect, but Derrick and my relationship was made of all the things that could and would sustain us through the good and bad times. We were perfectly imperfect, flawed and totally limited in our perception of marriage, yet I knew we could make it work. The foundation had been laid. All we had to do was stand in it, allow God to mold us, and to build the walls of unselfish love to cover us in peace.

Everything was set, the venue was exquisitely decorated. The menu had been planned, tasted, and set for a culinary experience our guests would not forget. The color theme complimented the progressive colors of pre-fall and echoed the sun's bouncing rays as the colors came alive at the announcement of sunset. The stage had been set, and the music had been cued up, the guest all seated among the rich hues of gold, cream, and the array of shades of burgundy flowers. The flickering light from the candles added to the ambiance and the anticipation of the days' event. There was a tranquil calm in the air. The bridesmaids had been primed, and the groomsmen were all robed in custom fitted tuxedos. They were coupled up as they walked down the aisle to the melodic tones of Brian McKnight's *"Never Felt This Way"*.

Everyone made their way down the long aisle past the smiling faces of guests. I wanted to take a peek, but my nerves kept me at bay. I waited. I closed my eyes, took a deep breath as the song ended and prepared to march to the beat of my heart like I had dreamed of some many times before. When the piano notes matched the beat of my heart, the wedding planner signaled for me to get ready for my entrance. The next song began to play, *"Still in Love"* by Brian McKnight, being sung by an exceptionally talented high school friend of mine, who had recently signed a record deal. Simultaneously the lace curtains were pulled back. I stood there in the middle of the entrance. Slowly I opened my eyes, looked down the flower laced path and caught Derrick's eyes. I locked on to him and allowed his smile, those dimples that I had fallen in love with, to guide me to him. My father and stepfather, one on each side of me, escorted us to the love of my life. I listened to the lyrics of the song as they reinforced why I loved Derrick so. In that moment, any nervousness, anxiousness, and doubt that lingered was gone. I knew with each step I took toward him; I knew I was right where I was supposed to be as Derrick lip-synced the words of the song, "I'll be still in love with you". I smiled, wanting him to prove it to me.

Both dads agreed to give me in love and wisdom to Derrick. There I stood before friends, family, and Derrick, willing to commit my life, my love, and soul to our marriage. The pastor started the service by having Derrick and I join hands. He told us from this point on, we were to become one, not in the physical sense but the way we moved, communicated, and our actions when it came to preserving the bond we were initiating today. That we both had a greater obligation to each other past the celebratory ceremony we were engaged in. That from this point forward, everything we did, every word we spoke, should reflect each other. That love should be the motivating factor in everything we do. Without love being the driving force, we leave no room for God's guidance in our marriage because he is love. Derrick and I stood there looking into each other's eyes. It was the image that created fairytales and the hope of love ever after. The pastor asked if we were ready to embark on love's journey, we both in unison said yes.

"Tracy, I Derrick Allen Montgomery pledge to give you the very best of me every day. To make you smile, to love you unconditionally, to forgive freely, to argue with you so we can make up, to grow with you, to cherish you, to wipe your tears, to hear your cries, to take away your stress, to provide protection, to take care of you, to be your friend, to strive to understand the most intimate parts of you, and to give you all the things you deserve.

You have been the light that illuminates my world. Your touch provides the warmth that covers me from the outside world and shelters me from pain. Your voice provides the wisdom and courage I need to conquer the world. It echoes the beat of my heart and keeps in sync with you. Your beauty shades out the distraction of this world and keeps me grounded. I thank you for allowing me to be the man who has the honor of keeping all of these treasures safe in my heart. I will guard and protect all that you mean to me with my life. I will not fail you, my love, I will love you until my dying day and even then, my love will live on. I love you now, tomorrow, and for all eternity. With this ring, I pledge my all to you." Derrick confidently spoke as he placed the ring on my left ring finger.

"Derrick, I have loved you since our first date. I knew right then and there that you were the only man for me. I knew I wanted to spend the rest of eternity, proving to you just how much I love you. I, Tracy Marie Scott, promise to be your peace, be your partner, build you up, offer support and encouragement, be a sounding board of positivity in a world that would tell you that you are not worthy. You are worth more than gold and for that you will be my king, the head of our household, not simply because you're a man. Still, because you have earned the right to lead me in all things, your love is unmatched and it drives me to want to be submissive, a proverbs woman, a Godly woman who will shower you with nothing less than the love that God has shown me. I want to be your one and only, your Alpha and Omega, the reason you smile, the cause of your laughter and the source of joy that will sustain you a lifetime. So, with this ring, I promise to love you today, tomorrow and for all eternity," I concluded as I placed the ring on Derrick's left ring finger.

We both smiled at each other. There was just one thing left to say and do. The pastor concluded the ceremony by uttering the words I had waited a lifetime to hear, "Derrick, you may now kiss your bride," and without hesitation, Derrick pulled me close to him. He placed his hand on my lower hip and one behind my neck and gently dipped me into a smooth kiss as I closed my eyes and savored the moment. His kiss sealed the deal. He kissed me long. He kissed me hard. Before

God, our family and friends, our commitment was sealed. I would prove to him that I could keep that vow. From this day forward, I would protect, cherish, honor and love him until my last breath. And with that kiss, I knew he would do the same. "I now present to you, Mr. and Mrs. Derrick Allen Montgomery" the pastor cheered. The congregation applauded and cheered as the beginning of our story book whirlwind romance began it's happily ever after.

I couldn't wait to write the chapters of our life together. I loved Derrick with my whole heart. He would always be the biggest part of me. I promised him I would love him forever, and forever starts today. I truly am the luckiest girl in the world. Life couldn't get any better than this moment, I thought to myself as Derrick and I walked down the aisle hand and hand, smiling through the crowd of family and friends cheering us on. We were married now, and I could not wait for our journey as husband and wife to begin.

The Present

Rebecca was enjoying every minute of being here with us. Matthew kept her occupied with being a grandmother. She looked at him with eyes of wonderment. I could tell that she saw bits and pieces of Derrick in Matthew. She would often gasp, smile, or shed a tear when he displayed certain behaviors. I saw her come alive. Maybe for the first time in her life, certainly since I had known her, Rebecca was living. Not the superficial, materialistic pretentious life she had created for herself. She had dropped all her pretenses, she had unmasked her armor, and allowed herself to be free of the socially approved norms and was just Rebecca. Maybe for the first time in her life, she didn't have to hide or pretend. I saw the change in her. I knew she felt it within herself.

I allowed Rebecca to accompany Matthew and me on my next OBGYN appointment. Just like Matthew, Rebecca beamed with excitement. Her reaction to seeing her unborn grandson twisting and turning inside my tight belly brought tears to her eyes. She held my hand as Matthew pointed out what he was doing on the monitor. She smiled. It was genuine and pure. Rebecca's life had changed within a matter of months. I could tell that the surprises that greeted her were beyond her expectations. She would now be the grandmother of two exceptional grandsons. Something she nor I ever saw coming. That is what made this so special. I was happy that she was here to witness this moment. She squeezed my hand and kissed me on the forehead. I looked up at her. This may have been the first mother daughter moment that we shared. It felt like she had kissed me for herself, Derrick, and my mom. I welcomed her expression of love. It was a memory that would replace all the nightmares that I had clung to all these years about Rebecca. It was the fresh start we both needed.

Rebecca and I took this time to become reacquainted. She shared intimate things with me that I could tell she needed to unpack. I, in turn, listened without judgement and provided the support she needed. Our Mornings became a welcome normal. We would joke and have moments of reflection. Our love brought us together for Derrick, but we realized that we had way more in common than just him. Our Quarantine conversations helped me to see the human side of a tortured soul. She had disguised her pain in pretty designer packaging. At the core she was just as vulnerable, scared, and helpless as we all were. I could clearly see why she had done what she did for Derrick. The only way she knew to protect him was the way she had protected herself. It was that denial that she had lived in for so many years. The only problem was she could only contain her denial. She had failed to share the rules of her game with Derrick.

As the days went by, Rebecca had made herself comfortable, and I comfortable with her being here. Who would have thought, enemies of the state would become allies. Rebecca helped around the house. She played tirelessly with Matthew and was finally taking her medications regularly. She was committed to the process. It wasn't something I brought up, but something Rebecca disclosed to me. She was finally owning who she was, had been, and who she wanted to become. She would no longer be defined by the stigma of mental illness. It was clearly a part of her, but it was not who she was. It was something I wished Derrick had reasoned. It was finally the example of a loving mother I had prayed she was for her son. It was also the moment I had to acknowledge that she was. Rebecca was the mother Derrick needed, and she did the best she could with what she knew. It was then that I realized that Rebecca wasn't the adversary I should have been fighting. She was a casualty of the same war I had fought in. I was simply happy that now I could provide the support and love she needed to will herself to health. Quarantine had provided the triage we both so desperately needed.

The Present

Dearest Tracy,

How is the most beautiful woman in the world doing today? In my mind, even among all the clutter, there will never be anyone that can match your beauty. There were nights that I would just watch you sleep and think to myself how lucky I was to have such a beautiful wife. Not just on the outside, but your soul was pure. You had a way of looking at the world that always gave me hope. Everyone who came into contact with you felt your beauty. It was just a part of your truth that made you so special.

So how are you? My Sons? Are you excited about the baby? Have you decided on a name? Tell me that our baby is growing and is healthy. What about Matthew? How is he adjusting? My Mother? I know I have all these questions, and I long to be in a place that I could hear your reply to all of this. I hope you don't mind me asking. I wish I could have this conversation with you in person. I never anticipated that I would not be by your side. That I would not hear your voice. The way you laugh at my corny jokes, or the side eye looks you would give me would not be part of my everyday mementos. I just want you to know that I do care. I did everything I could to be by your side right now. How I'd love to see you smile and the fact that my mind, these voices, these thoughts won't let me, won't allow me to be right there with you, at this moment, holding you, kissing you, loving you the way I promised. I thought if I could just tell you, if I could just make sure that you knew just how much... You would know I care more than words could express.

I imagine that you are happier than you have been in years. I hope that Matthew and my mother are filling our home with laughter and love. That they are replacing the stale air I suffocated you with and replacing it with the freshness that allows you to breathe clearly. I can see you smiling in my thoughts. I even hear your laugh. It gives me the inner peace I need. I know that you will be ok. Not with me being gone, but with the fact that you are happy and living again. Each day, I pray this journey becomes a little easier for you to travel. I'll be there in the background, silently cheering you on.

You are almost ready to give birth to our son. I'm excited for you and sad at the same time. I am excited because we are having a baby. A piece of both of us that will be the purest expression of the love we shared. It's a constant reminder that I am still there with you despite my absence. This is also the reason I'm so torn.

If I thought there was a better way, I'd find it. But I know as I write this letter that I won't be there. Everything that I can image will be the thoughts and dreams I make up. I will never experience the actual acts of any of the images in my mind. I'll never have the opportunity to hold my son. Hell, I don't even know his name. I'll never be there for any of his first. I'll miss out on sharing with him the things my father shared with me. I'll never be able to tease him, or Matthew, hear them laugh, and be there when they shed a tear. I prayed the voices in my mind would allow me the space and time to be there. Their aggression and cold-hearted words, trying to confuse me into thinking I am not worthy. That my sons are better off without me. They remind me daily of what I did to Jackson and I believe them. So, I'm no longer fighting their words. I'm so sorry Tracy.

I don't want to leave this message on a sad note. That was not my intention. So, don't worry about me. Remember I am there with you in the best parts. You lady, are the best part of me. I know the memories that you create now will be the ones you need. Rebecca, Matthew and our Son will make sure that you are taken care of. They will provide you the laughs, fun and love you need to undo everything that I did. They will show you the beauty in me and give you all the reasons to love again.

Look, I can tell you're smiling now! I also know the tears falling from your eyes are tears of joy because everything I just said is happening as you read this. I can finally smile because I *could not wish for anything more for you. Keep smiling, laughing and breathing. You deserve to live now. Let them give your life*

Loving you always,

Derrick

I just sat there in silence and allowed Derrick's words to marinate into my soul. I wanted to answer all of his questions. I wanted to tell him he was so worthy of the love I had come to know and experience from Matthew and his mother. That our son was healthy and getting better by the moment. That I wished he were here with me, to hold me and kiss me. That this journey would only be perfect if we could travel it together. I knew he would smile at my optimistic view of the world of him and I. The truth was I knew my words fell on deaf ears because my voice was mute compared to those that occupied his mind. But Derrick was getting the last laugh. He had found a way to let his light shine amid all the darkness that surrounded him. I knew his truth. I knew his heart. I knew the kind of man he was despite the picture his mental illness tried to paint. I would make sure our sons knew also.

The Present

I was up bright and early this Sunday morning. The aroma of bacon and warm maple filled the house like a scented candle. I always made a big deal out of Sunday breakfast. I would cook all of Derrick's favorite breakfast items. I would create a smorgasbord of tasty food for us to eat. He and I would nibble off of the abundance of food well past lunchtime. We would take our plates back to the bedroom and watch the pregame newscast for football. We would laugh and joke around. Plan our fantasy football league strategies. It was the perfect way to wind down our weekend and get ready for the hustle and bustle of our week. I guess jumping out of bed early on Sunday was just ingrained in me. Making a big breakfast had become a tradition I wasn't ready to let go of.

I sat at the breakfast nook, looking out the window. It was a beautiful crisp December morning. It was unusually warm for this time of the year. All week-long neighbors were putting up Christmas decorations without the threat of snow. There were still remnants of fall still scattered across the yard. I imagined watching Derrick out there cleaning up the leaves. The lawn was his pride and joy. A task that he readily accepted the moment we purchased the house. He kept it well-manicured. Derrick had mastered his horticultural calling from the grass to the ornamental hedges, the trimming of the mature oak that anchored the corner lot of our property. I imagined him waving to me as he walked by. I would smile and wave him in by holding up a cup of coffee. He would give me a nod and shortly, he would enter the backdoor, smelling like the great outdoors. I sat there waiting to hear the closing of the backdoor, listening for his footsteps, sniffing for the smell of leaves, grass, and the crispness of the air. I sat there waiting for him to come sit next to me and rub his hands across my thigh. I would twitch and laugh as he leaned in for a kiss. His warm lips would greet my lips, sending a chill down my spine. Imagined that one day I would feel this again. I imagined that one day, Derrick and I would see each other again out that window. And this time I wouldn't be so quick to hold back.

I reached down into the pocket of my robe for the next letter. I had placed it in there prior to coming downstairs to fix breakfast. I opened the envelope and pulled the folded paper out. I took a sip of my coffee as I began to read.

Hello Beautiful,

I'm writing this from one of your favorite spots in the house. I knew the moment that you saw the kitchen, this house was meant for you. Your eyes lit up like a child on Christmas morning. It was like the previous owners had designed this space with you in mind. When you ran to the kitchen nook and sat there staring out the window. You made up stories of all the things that would happen in our future around this table. You told of us having a family, growing old together with such vivid details that I believed you. I saw our present and future all in that moment. I just couldn't have predicted that life would throw us a speed bump along the way. This was the reason I knew we had to have this house. All because you saw this room as a place that we could have morning coffee, share stories, talk about our days, and raise our children in. I'm sitting here looking out the window imagining things had turned out just as you painted that image in my head. It was so vivid, so full of hope. Oh, how I wanted to give you all of that and more.

I'm looking out the window, looking back on all the memories that took place outside this window. The leaf fights, the picnics, the water balloon fights, the late-night star gazing, and the barbeques. We really did have some good times. Now I think about you and the boys creating your own memories. I close my eyes and think about you chasing them around outside. Imagine them talking you into getting a dog and the fun that happens with two boys and a puppy. I look out this window and wonder what they will be like. Will they be curious, athletic, or adventurous? I wonder how much of me will they inherit? I imagine pictures around the oak tree, leaf fights and water gun fights. I see bicycles and games of tag. Action figures and friends. I see both Matthew and our son being best friends. Even with the age difference, I just know that they will always have each other's back.

I never knew all the things you could see out of this window. It's almost magical. In this corner of the kitchen, you can see the entire house. It offers the most picturesque view of our property. How did

I not know this until now. Leave it up to me to uncover one of your hidden jewels when it's too late for us to enjoy it together. It is so peaceful sitting here. As I write this letter, I imagined you coming down the stairs to make your wonderful Montgomery Sunday breakfast spread. You, wearing your robe with your monogram initials on it. The one I purchased for you after we were married. Your hair up in a messy bun. I watch you walk down the stairs as you show a little side leg through the opening of the robe. Imagine underneath you're wearing the nude color lace bra and thong set. It was always my favorite. If I close my eyes really tight, I can smell the leftover scent of your perfume, Mon Paris over the warm maple syrup.

I sit here wondering if I'm as crazy as I am insane for leaving you. I promised you that I would love you forever. You will always be the biggest part of me. I just wish forever could last more than the present time. Looking out this window, I feel like forever could go on. That there are still memories that you and I can create. That we still have time to laugh, love and live. Isn't this how it should be? The reason I purchased this home for you so that that time would give us forever. I want to sit here in this moment, while my mind is quiet and tell you all the things I'll never have an opportunity to say. I want to joke with you. Hold you in my arms while I read to you. Sing, dance and live. But I know the noise will return shortly. I would trade anything to be able to create the memories you painted for me. I want them so bad. I want to stay here with you and the boys in this moment. Creating memories that I don't have to imagine. I wish you knew how much I want that with you. More memories and less agony. Less pain. Less heartache.

I now know why you sit here Tracy. In the still of the night when you can't sleep, in the rays of the morning sun. It's such a perfect seat. It is the window to our soul. It's the center of our home. You can see and be anything you need to be. Right now, I'm choosing to be the Derrick you love. The one you married, the keeper of your memories, your biggest fan, the one you adore, the love of your life. Even if things may have changed in reality, the voices distort my view and cloud you out. I want you to know I now know the secret. Whenever I'm feeling low, whenever I'm feeling lost. I hope it's ok if I sit in your seat. This window has the perfect view of everything I chose to remember about us. I hope and pray when you sit here, you think about only the good times. The peace within our home. The beauty within me.

Look out the window and see me. See me with a smile on my face. I know I'll always imagine you that way. You are sitting here sipping coffee, looking at me. Yea, that's the image I'll enjoy. The one when you smile at me, and I soon head into the house after you. I know the secret now Tracy. I just need to sit here and imagine.

Love you always,

Derrick

I dropped my cup of coffee. It spilled all over the floor. The cup shattered into pieces. My hand covered my mouth. I felt Derrick. He had sat here doing the same thing I was doing at this very moment. He knew. He remembered the memories we shared. He held on to them. Even when he couldn't voice them, even amid his war, he knew.

It was another victory; a battle won. I thought to myself, as tears flooded my face. Knowing we shared yet another memory, I smiled, and how my favorite spot in the house just became our favorite seat in the house. I would gladly share it with you Derrick. I grabbed the letter, placed it on my heart, and held it there. I sat there with yet another memory of you I would never forget.

The Present

———————— ❧ ————————

Weeks had turned into months, and Rebecca and I were still living under one roof. No stones had been thrown, no jabs taken, and no unkind words were spoken. Rebecca was making plans to relocate here to Kalamazoo. We had discussed what that would look like and we both agreed it was time. Rebecca wanted the opportunity to be a grandmother and I certainly could use the help. Besides, the motherly love she had shown me since she arrived was a welcome gift that had unwrapped itself and kept giving. We had hoped to have her move complete by the holiday season.

Rebecca would travel back and forth between here and her home in New York over the next couple of weeks. According to Rebecca, her adorable brownstone would be rented out to a young married couple that came from a good family, which I took to mean that they had the pedigree and money to afford the comforts of life to Rebecca's standards. The hired movers had managed to pack up the Montgomery Brownstone. Whatever Rebecca refused to sell had made its way to Michigan. Derrick and I had assumed that this day would come for one of our mothers or fathers. The day one or maybe both would have to move into our home due to old age or health concerns. We had discussed choreographing the efforts on what this would mean for our family and the need for additional space. So, Derrick planned ahead.

Derrick had the garage remodeled to include a small studio apartment above the car port. The studio consists of a bedroom, full bathroom, living room, and a small kitchenette area. The gally style kitchen was just big enough for a small refrigerator and stove. The studio had an outside entrance for privacy, with an entrance from the second-floor hallway of the main house. Rebecca loved the idea of not being a burden, and I like the idea of her having her own space. As soon as the moving truck arrived, the movers were instructed by Rebecca like a drill sergeant. She knew where each item that made the long haul from New York to Michigan was to be placed. I stayed out of the way from the hustle and bustle of men coming in and out and the skilled dictatorial voice that ushered from Rebecca as she gave direction.

The movers had finally departed. Rebecca had been absent from Matthew and I all day. It was 8 pm when Rebecca finally emerged from her new home. She called Matthew and I from the upstairs balcony. We both rushed to see what the commotion was all about.

"It's finally ready", Rebecca boasted as she waved us both upstairs and led the way down the hallway.

Matthew and I followed close behind her. Rebecca opened the door to her apartment and for the first time, I could see Derrick's plan come to life. I wasn't sure about the studio apartment when he first told me about his plan. It seemed like a waste of money and space. Especially when we have more than enough bedrooms to accommodate everyone, he would just tell me to believe in the process. So, I did. Even when the space went unoccupied for years, I didn't say a word. But it didn't mean I forgot about the money spent on the remodel. But now, it had all come together. I realized his vision for what this day would look like. The need to offer independence and comfort while providing safety and closeness to family. I was finally able to see his plan in action.

Rebecca had decorated the studio to make it her own. She had the walls painted. Her artwork adorned the walls and provided the charm and character she needed to make it feel as close to New York as possible. Everything was perfectly placed. She even had a wooden electric fireplace with mantel stationed in the corner of the Livingroom. It resembled the fireplace that we used to gather around at her home in New York. It was Rebecca in every way. It was beautiful. This was what Derrick had envisioned. A place for his mother to have; a place to call her own without feeling like a burden. She would be close to us and still have her privacy. It was home. I hugged Rebecca and smiled as she showed Matthew and I around her new place. She beamed with pride. Knowing how pleased Derrick would have been, I smiled that this moment had finally come, and his plan realized. It was one of the many things I wished I could tell Derrick he had gotten right.

The Present

The Holiday season was in full swing. I was in my final month of pregnancy and feeling the weight of carrying this baby. From the backaches and the swollen feet, I was ready to give birth and control my body back. I had given up control of a few things and allowed Rebecca to take the reins. She wasted no time with taking over managing the household. She had Matthew up early and had hired a private tutor to get Matthew ready for first grade. Under Rebecca's watch, Matthew spent about two hours each morning learning math, science, and English with his tutor. He was already reading at a second-grade level and understood basic math problems. Rebecca wanted to make sure it stayed that way and spared no expense making sure Matthew was prepared for his future education. Their relationship gave me insight to how Rebecca managed Derrick's education. It helped me appreciate his love for knowledge even more, knowing that his mother helped cultivate that thirst within him.

Rebecca also made sure the home was immaculately decorated. Rebecca had dressed the house in a cream and gold themed holiday display of lights, tasteful decorations, and Christmas trees throughout the home. It certainly made the home feel festive. It had Matthew all geared up to open up presents even though we were weeks away from Christmas. Yes, Rebecca had managed to bring a little cheer into the home. As much as I wanted to smile, there was a void attached to the season of hope. I missed Derrick. This was the first Christmas I would spend without him. And while it was a first of many positive things, it was Derrick that I had hoped would also be by my side to share in these moments. While Rebecca and Matthew shared making the home as festive and bright as they could, I found myself participating more in exclusion in search of solitude.

It was in moments like this that I needed to hear Derrick's voice. I needed to be reminded of why. I was starting to think that all of this was too much for me to bear. There was no way I would be able to be a mother to two small children without him. There was no way I could ever have my career and still manage this house and be a mother. I just couldn't do it without Derrick. Not without his support and love. What had I gotten myself into? How was I ever going to make sense of all of this? I was way too far along to have this kind of doubt, and yet, here I was swimming neck deep into unchartered water. I felt like the lone seaman in a raft amid high tides and rough winds.

I tried really hard to get into the mood. Rebecca and Matthew were trying their best to bring the holiday cheer alive. I would crack a half smile, even sing along with some of the music Rebecca had on constant replay in the evenings, but none of it brought a lasting emotion of joy. The more I tried to hide it, the more it began to show. Even in my last session with Dr. Mary, I had expressed my overwhelming feelings of sadness with her. Dr. Mary had expressed that many people experience depression around the holidays. Missing Derrick had become a trigger for me, especially since everything else in my life had started to manifest itself in such a positive way. She asked me if I was feeling guilty. At first, I didn't understand the question. But the more she explained to me my circumstances, the more it began to make sense.

I couldn't enjoy my life right now because I was feeling guilty about my life with Derrick, specifically the final months of this life. I had lived in the should've, could've, would've stage of grieving. I had wondered if I had done something different, that maybe he would be here. I started to blame myself for all the things I didn't do and should've done. Dr. Mary had helped me self-discover that there was nothing I could have done to change the outcomes that lead Derrick to take his life. No amount of reliving the events, the pain, or dreadful guessing game, would undo the pain and despair that Derrick was in. We don't if a kinder word, a more loving act, or me being more empathetic would have altered the events that took place in March. Blaming myself was not the answer to something I could not change. If not in March, maybe April, maybe later this year, maybe next, who knows, but at some point, Derrick would try to take his life. It was the nature of his mental illness. It had broken him down and made him feel worthless. In turn, it had made me an unwilling victim, and now had played on my emotions. I had almost believed that I too, was unworthy of the life and the love I was given.

Dr. Mary suggested a few exercises for me to practice this holiday season. I was more than willing to try out her advice. The most powerful thing she expressed to me during our last session of 2020 was the minute I start to feel sad and want to isolate myself, that would be the moment you draw closer to Matthew and Rebecca. Stay in their presence and be open to receiving the love they are offering you. I shook my head and agreed. It was the least I could do. Besides, Derrick's mental illness had already taken one victim, but it would not take me too.

The Present

I had survived my first Christmas without Derrick, thanks in no small part to Matthew and Rebecca. We were up bright and early as the excitement of the holiday took over an eager Matthew like a possessed doll. Before the sounds of snowplows could be heard clearing away the first signs of winter, and the darkness of winter solace echoed the coming of dawn, Matthew was up. He was up and wide awake and he made sure that he was not alone. Matthew scampered from bedroom to bedroom, waking me up first and then walking down the hall and into Rebecca's apartment and knocking vigilantly on her bedroom door. His sweet voice guided both Rebecca and I to "come on," as he ran down the stairs and waited patiently.

Rebecca had truly out done herself. The Christmas tree had been stocked high with gift after gift. Not only had she played her own Santa, but she made sure that Matthew, baby Montgomery, and I all had reasons to smile this morning. It was completely unexpected, extravagant, and welcomed. Rebecca believed that after the year we had, we all deserved the right to smile this Christmas, and no expanse was spared. Matthew was in heaven as he opened gift after gift. He was calling out the items as if Rebecca and I could not see the toys for ourselves. When it was my turn, Matthew brought my gifts over to me. My now protruding belly and swollen feet made even the smallest movements a task. Matthew even helped me tearing open some gifts because he assumed I was taking too long. Before we knew it, the family room had been covered with torn wrapping paper, emptied boxes, and a mass array of gifts all needing a designated spot within the house.

I did however manage to cook a family Christmas ham dinner for the three of us to enjoy. The small seven-pound ham was more than enough for us to eat. I was hoping that the leftovers would give Rebecca and I a day off from cooking. The ham was accompanied by candied yams, steamed cabbage, wild rice, baked macaroni and cheese, sweet dinner rolls, ambrosia salad, a sweet potato pie, cookies, and a pecan pie. It truly was enough food to feed a small army. I wanted to make sure that Rebecca and Matthew knew how much I appreciated everything they had done and what they meant to me. Truth be told, I was worn out and maybe had done just a little too much. I was feeling the effects of my drained energy and needed to rest. Matthew must have felt the same as he had fallen asleep on the floor, surrounded by all his new toys.

Rebecca wasn't far behind. I noticed her dozing off from the corner of my eyes. I wrapped her and Matthew up in the chenille throws that were housed in the family room chest. They were both resting well after a morning of excitement that started well before daybreak. I watched from the kitchen as her head took a slight tilt and her eyes rolled back. She was tired and rightly so. Rebecca had been moving non-stop since she arrived. It was time she rested. I was happy that she was comfortable enough to do so in this household. I was pleased that she wanted a permanent place in my family. So, Rebecca closing her eyes was well overdue.

I took this moment of solitude to read one of the final letters from Derrick. I had taken the unopened envelope out from the remaining stack. The next letter was marked differently from the previous letters. It said not to open until delivery date. I wondered what could have been so important that Derrick wanted me to wait. As much as I wanted to read Derrick's thoughts, I respected his wishes and waited. I placed the letter in my hospital bag that was packed and placed by the backdoor. Now that my plans had been derailed, I found myself wanting to take a nap as well. Dinner was done and the house was finally cooling off from the oven being on all morning. The coolness from the dropping temperatures outside made the house a perfect temperature for resting. I made my way into the family room, grabbed a blanket from the chest, and cuddled up in the leather recliner, joining the rest of my family in sleep.

The Present

—— ∿ ——

I had survived Christmas with my new family. Unlike years past, Christmas was a chore that I dreaded participating in. Rebecca's presence used to numb my soul, and Derrick's unpredictable behavior dimmed my light. I viewed the attending of holiday office parties with the same fate as feeding me Castrol oil as a kid, a necessary evil. The fake smiles, the shaking of hands of those I suspected could not be careless of about the reality of Derrick and my true-life story. It was all for show and appearances. As long as my presence equated to dollar signs, corner office and VP status, then my job was done. After all, I needed something in return for all the chaos and heartache I had endured. But this year was different. This year I had experienced loss in the most horrible of ways. I had to stop playing the victim and own my role in the downfall of my marriage. I had to admit that I was not the person I thought I was and be comfortable with the woman I am now. I opened my heart to love in the hardest way possible. And I've had to learn to forgive truly and freely, which is not so easy for a

Capricorn to do. This Christmas was nothing like years past, but it was everything I want my holidays to be in the future.

I had just laid Matthew down to sleep. Rebecca had just retired to her suite, and I was turning in for the night. I made sure the security alarm had been set and that all the lights were turned down, the doors were all locked, and the kitchen was cleaned. I was heading up the stairs when all of a sudden, a streak of pain ran up my back. I grabbed my stomach and held on to the stair rail. I waited a few seconds, caught my breath, and attempted to move further up the stairs. I made it up to three more stairs before the next painful streak. I breathed and caught myself on the stairs. I was used to Braxton Hicks contractions, but the pain and the quickness of the pain I was experiencing signaled this may be more than that.

I held on tight to the stair rail as I made my final attempt to make it up the stairs. I took a step up the riser, and a warm gush of liquid poured out of me as if I had accidentally peed myself. I let out a muttered scream as the pain intensified and crippled me. I sat there on the steps catching my breath and trying to gain control of the situation. I breathed through the pain, clinching onto the railing.

"REBECCA!" I yelled out in pain. "REBECCA!" I yelled once more while catching my breath.

I waited on the stairs as contraction after contraction hit me like a bolt of lightning.

Realizing that Rebecca may not hear me thru the sound barrier of the hallway and the closed door, I immediately started calling for Matthew. With the next two contractions, I held on tight to the railings and held myself and breathed through them. The frequency of the contractions was alarming. I didn't have a watch on and couldn't see the kitchen clock from my position on the stairs, but I knew that the contractions were happening well within the three-minute mark. I took the time in between the contractions to slide down the stairs. I knew there was no way I would be able to make it to the top of the staircase. I made it down the stairs and hit the home alarm system.

Today

I awoke to find myself in the hospital. The last thing I could recall was hearing the cries of my newborn son. I was attached to a slow drip saline IV and an oxygen mask. The heart monitor was fixed on my index finger. Where was Rebecca and Matthew? Where was my baby? I began to panic. Before I could push the nurse call button, in walked a female dressed in scrubs. I could assume she was either a nurse or nurse's aide. She was wearing a mask, but her eyes were warm and comforting.

"You're awake" she stated.

I shook my head yes. She went on to introduce herself to me as she took my vitals. I waited patiently for her to finish before I attempted to remove the oxygen mask off my face.

"Just wait one moment and I will remove that for you" she insisted. "After I'm done with this, would you like for me to bring your son to you?" she asked.

I shook my head yes and answered her at the same time.

She handed me a surgical mask to place over my mouth and nose. I adjusted my bed so that I was sitting up. I took a look around the room. There were balloons and flowers. The door opened and Anna the nurse was pushing a rolling plastic baby carriage. Tucked inside all swaddled, up was my son. She pushed the carriage closer to me. I could feel my heart beating. According to the date on the whiteboard, I had missed almost a day of bonding with him. I wanted to hold him. I needed to see him.

The nurse must have sensed my impatience. She reached down into the sterile plastic bassinette and picked up my son and laid him in my arms with care. I exhaled, taking in this moment. I almost forgot to breath. I was at a still. The last time I had been in this place was with Jackson. I held my sweet boy for all of five minutes before his lifeless body was whisked away and Derrick and I were forced to sign the death certificate before the shock of what just happen was realized. I wasn't sure what to do next. It was all so surreal. I had waited nine months, pleaded insanity, lost my best friend and gained a whole new reason for living when most people would have just given in. It was all too much to endure in less than a years' time. 2020 had dealt me a shitty hand that I was forced to play. I was losing with every card drawn and yet I won.

It didn't seem fair. Nothing about this year or my life seemed reasonable. The year's chaotic start was finishing with the calmness and beauty of me holding my dear son. I looked down at him. He was a perfect ending for a broken heart. He laid in my arms as if he knew I was his mother. My heartbeat was in sync with his. His eyes were closed; his cheeks were flushed. He was swaddled and nestled in my arms. The nurse had asked if I needed anything. I just shook my head no. I couldn't take my eyes off of him. I just held him. I held him for both me and Derrick. A million thoughts rushed through my mind. But as soon as he opened his eyes and looked up to me, all the worry and fear subsided. I was in love. I was loving unconditionally for the first time in my life. The innocence that had escaped me had resurfaced not once but twice. I had finally won. And the prize was greater than anything I could have imagined.

Rebecca and Matthew had made their way up to the hospital. I knew they had visited earlier while I was sleeping. This time they were able to visit with me while the baby was up. Matthew jumped right into an older protective brother role. He had instructed Rebecca to wash her hands and put hand sanitizer on before touching his brother. He watched with a keen eye all the hospital staff that entered the room. He was making sure that they did not do anything to upset me or his brother. He was cute. But I also knew that much of his experience and distrust of hospitals may have come from his previous experience with his biological mother. I reassured him that we were ok. I even had him come sit next to me on the bed so that he could watch up close everything the nurses were doing.

Rebecca was the first to hold the baby. She was so excited. She held him as if he were hers. I could see the tears swelling up in the corners of her eyes. Much like the feelings she had when she first met Matthew, Rebecca was holding on to the memories of her dear son. Derrick had a legacy that Rebecca didn't even know he left behind and here she was, able to nurture and watch over his legacy. It was the redemption she so desperately needed. The gift she needed and an opportunity for her to get it right this time. Rebecca just sat there, smiling. It was moments like this that I felt lucky to have her with me.

Rebecca and Matthew took pictures on the iPhone of the baby. They had pictures of each one of them holding him, me holding him, Rebecca and her grandsons, Me with my boys. We were creating memories that I wished Derrick could have been a part of. The room was filled with love. We were all drawn together because of him. There should have been at least one picture of Derrick with his son. With each snapshot, I took mental pictures. One so I'd never forget this moment, the others so that I could send them in prayer to Derrick.

Rebecca and Matthew had finally left for the evening. We had dinner together. They stayed while I washed the baby up, feed him, and put him to sleep. We kissed each other goodbye and confirmed what time they could come to visit tomorrow. They left the hospital room but not before Matthew whispered, he loved me and his baby brudda. I whispered back that I loved him too. The door closed behind them and I was alone again just as the day had began.

At that time, I remembered the letter that Derrick had requested be open at the birth of our son. I walked over to my overnight bag and grabbed the envelope that was tucked away. I was nervous and scared to read his thoughts. Unlike many of his letters previously, I knew that this letter made everything real. I had given birth to our son without him. I was in this alone. Something we had promised I would not go through by myself. It signified the end of Derrick and me. I knew from this way forward; I would be walking alone. That everything I would do; It would be just me. Yeah, I had Rebecca's help, but I would be alone in raising them when it came to those boys. I was a married, single parent. Something Derrick knew too. And his thoughts would echo those sentiments in his letter. I was sure of it.

My dearest Tracy,

You did it! You did it! I'm so proud of you. I wish I could be there with you. I also know that I've broken yet another promise I made to you. I'd apologize for not being there, but I can't. I can't apologize for removing myself from you and our boys. I was the single common denominator that posed a threat to you all. So, I COULDN'T BE THERE! I don't think you'll understand my reasoning, nor do I expect you to, but this was my choice. It was the only way I could make sure that I didn't harm you or them, ever.

I pray that he is healthy. I'm closing my eyes and picturing you holding him in your arms. I imagine myself holding him. That he looks up at me with your eyes, and that he loves me unconditionally despite my flaws and imperfections. I think about watching you love him the way you would have loved Jackson. How I took all those hopes and dreams away from you, and almost left you with nothing to replace them with. I think about what he looks like. If he and Matthew share any of my physical characteristics. Do they have my eyes, my dimples, my height? I also think that if they inherited my flaws. Did I pass my mental illness on to them? It's the most single doating question I have.

I prayed every day that God makes them pure. I asked that he lay their burdens on me. I pray that God's mercy does not make them pay for the sins of their father. I pray that this curse does not touch them. I pray for you and them. I would never want to have them follow in my footsteps and have them break your heart the way I did. I would never want you to become my mother and allow your love for them to mask the help they need. Or be the excuse for why they need assistance, but you try to fix them on your own because of your love. It is a battle you could never win. I wouldn't want you to have to try again, the way you did with me. If you couldn't make the difference for me, I find it hard to believe that you'll have success loving them to health. I imagine that they are nothing like me and yet be the best parts of me for you to hold on to.

I wish I were normal. I wish that I could be there by your side. I wanted to be there to coach you through the labor pains. I had missed so much of the opportunity with Jackson, listening to the voices in my head. I often think that had I been stronger, had I not been so weak of a man, things would be different. I wish that the voices in mind knew how much I wanted to be there. To be a husband and a father. But they don't care. And the helplessness I feel doesn't leave me with much to hold onto, other than their harsh criticisms of me. They have been both right and wrong about their assessment of me. And now I can't tell my rights from wrongs from listening to them for so long. I wish they could see what I see and allow me the future I promised you.

I'm envisioning your future. One without me. As difficult as it may be, you got this. You'll be the mother I knew you would be. They will grow to love and respect you. You'll adore and spoil them. It's just who you are. You'll be just what they need. No, it won't be easy all the time, but you'll handle it with grace. You'll grow to have it all. The career that you've worked so hard for if you should choose, and the children you've always wanted. You'll just have to do it without me. If I thought there was any other way, I wouldn't leave you alone to manage this difficult task. You're the strongest woman I know. You can handle it. All of it, and you'll do fine.

What I imagine most about this moment is that you know just how much I love you. Nothing will ever be more gorgeous to me than you being pregnant. And now that you're a mom, a mother to a son we made out of love, nothing could ever top the reasons I love you and only you. I can't put into words the feeling I have right now. It's one of completeness. Like now that I know you are taken care of, that you have surrounded yourself with everything I couldn't give you, and yet you have the best parts of me with you. I feel like I've done everything I needed to do, to right all of my wrongs. That's it, I finally feel complete. You Tracy Montgomery, complete me.

Congratulations sweetheart on having my baby. It truly means the world to me. You will forever be my lady. And when I close my eyes, I will always see you. I will always imagine the first time we met, the day of our wedding, and the image of you being pregnant. It is all I need. In this moment of silence, in the calmness of my mind, I clearly see you. I love you Tracy and I'm so honored to have been your husband and the father of our sons.

My Baby had my Baby, what a beautiful gift. What a lovely memory I'll never have.

Derrick

The Present

A few weeks had passed. We had celebrated the New Year as a new family unit. I was starting to create memories, beautiful memories of the new family I've created. Rebecca had become the endearing mother and loving grandmother. Matthew had made his way into my heart. His unconditional love was the medicine that I needed. He had shown me that I could love again. No, he wasn't my biological son, but he was mine. I would love him as if he were created just for me. His love made me forget the ills in which he was created. He made me see the beauty in the chaos that caused me so much heartache. Derrick Jr, or DJ as we called him, was the apple of my eye. He was the perfect gift I didn't see coming. In the midst of unspeakable grief, Derrick had left me with the sweetest present, our son. The fact that he did it on purpose, the fact that in the middle of our turmoil, we found time to make love with no regrets, we created something so precious, a perfect reflection of our union we never thought we would achieve. We were a family, and I wouldn't trade this or them for anything.

Derrick Jr. was growing fast. He looked every bit like Derrick. I must have been super upset with Derrick because everything Derrick Jr did resembled his father. And yes, he had Derrick's dimples. Matthew loved being a big brother. He would read to DJ, sing to him, and even slept in the room with him. They were two peas in a pod. I am going to enjoy watching them grow up together. I also knew I was going to have to watch them. Those dimples they inherited, and their boyish charm was sure to be a lady killer when they got older. After all, they were their father's sons. I just loved their relationship. I knew deep down that Derrick would have loved it too.

With each passing day, I became more efficient in tackling the role of a single parent. I was handling business and managing the needs of the boys. Thank goodness Rebecca was here to help. Not only was she an active grandmother, but she was becoming a friend to me as well. Our candid conversations, jokes, and cattiness were comforting, especially since we were still in the middle of the pandemic. But it was in the small moments that I came to appreciate Rebecca the most. Like when she could sense I was missing Derrick, her gentle motherly touch or smile made it alright to feel those feelings, but also told me I wasn't alone. Her kindness was an attribute I had failed to see through all the pain and grief. It was something she was unwilling to show for fear of being judged. But now, her kindness was who I had come to know, love, and respect.

We all celebrated by having Rebecca and Matthew make a cake and dinner for me on my birthday. It was a small intimate celebration. It was just the four of us; I didn't need much more than that. I wasn't expecting any gifts, so when the doorbell rang, and I answered it, the UPS driver had left a medium size box at my doorstep. It was addressed to me. There wasn't any return address or name. I placed it on the counter and proceeded to open the box. Inside there was a card that read, To My Dearest Wife, I hope you enjoy this gift as much as I enjoy seeing you smile. Happy Birthday, Derrick. The tears began to stream down my face. Rebecca rushed over to see what was going on. She pulled out the contents of the box. There were three individually wrapped boxes, each with a Tiffany blue ribbon.

The first box had a diamond tennis bracelet in it. I was beautiful. I had wanted a new tennis bracelet for the longest time. I had lost the first one Derrick had purchased for me while on a trip to the Bahamas. That was over seven years ago. I just never could see the reason for spending that much money on a piece of jewelry due to my carelessness. The next box had a pair of diamond earrings that matched the bracelet perfectly. They must have been about a carat each. The last box had a diamond necklace that had the birthstones of Derrick, Jackson, Matthew, and Derrick Jr surrounding the diamond. It was all too much. It was so unexpected. Derrick had put a lot of thought into this gift. Rebecca took the necklace and placed it around my neck. I rushed to the downstairs bathroom to take a look at what it looked like. It complimented my skin tone and sparkled like the stars in the night. I felt blessed that even with everything he must have been dealing with, he thought of me.

I helped clean up the kitchen and put the boys down for the night. Rebecca and I had a cup of hot tea, before calling it a night. I decided I would read one of the few remaining letters that Derrick had written to me. I was down to the last three letters. I was trying to stretch them out but found myself needing to hear his voice. I was running out of options. I had kept his cellphone active so that I could hear his message. I still had a few messages saved from when he called me. He sounded so happy and alive. Little did I know, it was all a mask he wore. I'm sure he had some good days and bad days, but when I hear his voice, all I hear is the good in Derrick. I feel his warmth. I see his smile, and I hear his contagious laugh that drew me even closer to him. I longed to hear that, to feel that, and would give anything to see it again, and I thought to myself as I clutched the necklace from Derrick that draped my neck.

Beautiful Tracy,

I hope that life is going well. I would be lying if I said I hope you're living your life the way you dreamed. The truth is, I know that you can't do that as long as I'm here. In order for you to live, love, and grow, I need to let you go. This is the hardest thing I have ever had to do. Lord knows when I saw you for the first time, I wanted to hold on tight to you. I never dreamt that we would ever be apart. And when you agreed to love me forever, I didn't imagine that forever would be just a few short years. But it is time.

At first, your love scared me. I didn't want to fall in love. I didn't really have the time. I had plans, big plans. I was going to conquer the world, but then you came along. You changed me; you made living worthwhile; you gave me purpose. I began to see that loving the right person was worth having you in my life. Because of you, I had it all. I can't imagine my life without you. I can't breathe without you. Everything I do or did was because I loved you as twisted as it may seem now.

As twisted as it may seem, I lived up to my vows the best way I could. Every day I tried to put you and your needs first. My passion in life was to see you smile. I wanted to dance with you, dream with you, and hold you in my arms and never let go. I know it may seem like I fell short of those expectations, but I didn't. I knew you dreamed of having a family. And while the family you have now is not the traditional family you thought you wanted, it's the one you needed. I danced with you every chance I got. Even up till the moment I left you and departed this life, we danced. I held you in my arms then and even now. I can feel the warmth of your body wrapped around me. Not a night went by that I didn't hold you if we were next to each other. Even when you didn't want me to, I did. I would hear you moan in your sleep when I placed my arms around you. You would melt into me and I would kiss your neck.

I also lived up to the other parts of my vows. I promised to protect you even if it was from myself. I said I would lay down my life to make sure you were ok and that was a price I needed to pay in order to make sure you would be fine. It was the hardest thing I had to do, but I loved you enough to know, I would cause you more harm than good. I don't blame you. I blame myself for not being strong enough to control the parts of me that prevented me from protecting you the way you wanted me to.

Maybe for the first time in my life, I can see and hear things clearly. Maybe it's because I am at peace with what happens next. Leaving you is the last thing I want to do, but it's a necessary evil. I also know what I'm about to ask you is a betrayal of everything I stood for at the altar. It goes against everything I promised you, and you promised me. It's the last favor I will ever request of you. It's the only one that matters. It's time. I need to let you go. You need to let me go. This will be the last letter I will write to you. I have no right to lay claim to your heart anymore. I need you to move on. I need you to find the love of a man that will love you all the ways I couldn't. I need you to be at peace with what was and remember us for what we were. I need you to forgive yourself and forgive me.

What we had was something so special. It was perfect for the time we spent together. Our love was genuine, honest, and pure. It was the love fairytales are made of. It's the kind of love people will look back and try to emulate. We were two people who were made to love each other, even if it wasn't the eternity we had hoped for. But all things come to an end. Even our story has an ending. As I write this letter, we are writing our ending. Through all the pain, confusion, chaos, drama, and hurt, the rainbow still shines on us. Look at you. Look at the legacy I get to leave behind. What a story you can tell. The narrative isn't so dark after all. Once the clouds were lifted, the sun came out and poured out its magnificent rays of hope and love upon you. The glow up that surrounds you is magnificent. It's time for you to shine now.

If there was one wish I'd make for you Tracy, it would be that you continue to love. Past the motherly love, past the love you had for me, but that you love again freely, without hesitation. There is someone out there waiting to know the love of a good woman. Some lucky bastard that needs to share and experience what you brought to my life. Just like me, he won't be looking for it, but when he finds you, he will want to hold on to you and never let you go. He will love you unconditionally. He will want to dance with you, share memories with you, and give you the world. And you need to allow him to do that. Make space for him. I already know your heart has the capacity to do so. There is space for all of us. Just look at the place you made for Matthew. There is room Tracy, allow him in. You deserve it.

The last two letters in the group are for the boys. I thought it would be time for me to speak to them. I know they are young now and will have questions. I want to be the one to answer them. You are already carrying the weight of two parents, so the least I could do is muster up the courage to face my sons. Besides, I can still share some things with them that only a dad can teach them. Please read the letters to them until they are old enough to read the letter on their own. After that, my burden will be lifted off your shoulders. Can you do that for me? Will you grant me this last wish? I have no right to ask, but I desperately need this from you. Then you will be absolutely free of me. Free to live your life.

Tracy, one last thing before I go. Close your eyes. Come on, close them. Imagine a world where mental illness doesn't exist, but just you and me. Our favorite Brian McKnight song is playing in the background. We dance. I hold onto you. You smell so good. I hear your heartbeat as it matches mine. The song never ends, and you and I have forever together. That's where I'll be when you need me. In that thought right there.

Did I make you smile? I sure hope so.

I love you Tracy Montgomery. It's always been you. Only you. Now go live your life. Live it as freely and as unapologetically as you can. Smile often and enjoy the memories we shared, but create new ones, often.

I'll see you on the other side.

Loving you always

Derrick.

The Future

Months turned into years. They eventually found a cure for Covid-19. The new normal became just that; normal. The world went on. Everyone carried on life as if nothing really happened. But I knew differently. I started 2020 on a high. Little did I know, that year would change my life forever.

I carried out Derrick's last wishes. I read the letters he left for the boys. Matthew and I read the letter every week. It served as a great way for him to increase his reading skills. I read to him for a few months and before long, he was reading the letter to me. I read Derrick Jr. his letter weekly also. It's funny because Derrick even called him DJ. It was like he knew I would name him after his father, even though he made mention to me that he never wanted to name his son after him. I read the letter to Derrick Jr. for the first four years of his life before he requested to read it on his own. I shared stories about Derrick with the boys and painted the picture of the type of man he was for them. I kept the drama out of it. I believed that our drama was for us to go through, not them to relive.

With each passing year, they grew up. Both looking more and more like Derrick. They both had his characteristics and mannerisms. It was almost like they were twins just born years apart. By the time Matthew was ten, he had started to receive a handwritten letter from Derrick yearly. The only thing I could think of was that he had arranged with his lawyer to send out the letters to the boys when the time came. DJ started to receive his letters at the age of seven. Like clockwork on their birthdays, Derrick's letters arrived. At first, I wanted to know what he said to them. All those years reading to them, Derrick's thoughts kept me tied to him. I could still hear him and held him close to me. But I knew those letters were the private conversation that fathers had with their sons. It was the conversations they would miss out on because of Derrick's absence. It only came once a year, but the way the boys read them, I was sure it contained information and insight that would last a lifetime. It was the ultimate love letter from a father to his sons.

By the time the boys were both teenagers, the letters had turned into video messages. After years of reading their father's thoughts, they could now hear his voice and see him. I remember when the first one arrived for Matthew. He cried. All this time, all he had were the pictures around the house and the memories I shared with him about Derrick. And now, here he was speaking directly to Matthew. At first, we thought the letters stopped. But like magic, they started to receive emails addressed to them at the family email address. The family email was something Derrick had set up when we had Jackson. Once I lost Jackson, we had rarely used that email address, but I still received alerts on items sent to that email. It was supposed to be a way to communicate with family. I would forward the videos to the boy's private account. I did so without looking. It wasn't my place.

I could tell they were soaking up everything that Derrick would say to them. DJ started using some of the same verbiages that Derrick used. They would even share things that their dad told them about me. It made me feel special that he thought of me even when he was trying to share those precious moments with his sons. I never asked about what they spoke about or what Derrick said. I just allowed them that peace of mind and moments that they shared with Derrick. Matthew and DJ would often share videos and letters with each other, but I never asked to be a part of their bonding time with Derrick. It was something that they shared together, that deepened their bond as brothers.

By the time they were twenty-one, the letters had slowed down. They only came on special events like graduation from college and wedding dates. But through the years, the boys kept all the communications they received from Derrick. I think weirdly, Derrick's form of parenting worked. It certainly gave them an opportunity to get to know him in ways I could not provide for them. I like to think that whatever he told them, helped mold them into the men they are today. They truly are the best parts of Derrick.

Rebecca had lived for ten more years with us, until her health took a bad turn. Not only was her mental health deteriorating, but when you add in Alzheimer's, it was just a matter of time. She always stated that she didn't want to be a burden, and the truth is she wasn't. It was my pleasure to stand by her side and nurse her just like any daughter would her mother. Right up till the end, Rebecca spoiled her grandsons. It was no surprise that the majority of her estate was left to them. I was surprised that she even left me a portion of her wealth. The inheritance was a welcomed gift, but the true blessing was having her here with us. The love and kindness that she brought into our lives was worth more than the money she left us. I know I would gladly trade it all in to have her and Derrick back with us if that was even possible.

What I missed most about Rebecca was our early morning and late-night tea talks. It was in those moments that I saw the real her. She was a mother, a grandmother, a wife, and a friend. I had seen her play all these roles at varying stages of her life. The one that stands out most to me is our friendship. It may have started out rocky, even turbulent at times. But in the end, she was my closest and dearest friend. We had shared so much in common, many of which we wished we hadn't. I guess that is what made us such a perfect pair. She understood me and I her, and when we stopped judging each other, we saw each other for who we were, just two women loving the same man and wanting the best for him. I was so happy that I had the chance to know that part of her. The memories I have of our time together, I will treasure forever.

I buried Rebecca right next to her son. I thought she would have loved that. I knew that if they were together, she could tell him all about his sons. She might even mention me.

Throughout the years, the one thing I did do was make sure the boys got tested. I know that this was something Derrick had mentioned in his letters to me. I also knew that mental illness is hereditary. I prayed that it would skip over them. I prayed that my genes and Matthew's mother's genes were dominant. That they would erase any notion of mental illness out of this family lineage. They were tested annually as a precaution. Unfortunately, fate would play a cruel joke on my heart once more. One of the boys began to show signs of the family trait as a teenager. But with medication and proper supervision, we controlled it. He managed it and knew the importance of why everything he had to do was necessary.

At first, I panicked. Worry had set in, and I began to relive everything that happened with Derrick. But I also knew I had educated myself on their mental illness. I had attended seminars, read books, and spoke to doctors about the condition. I was as prepared and better prepared than with Derrick. I would not allow what happened to him, happen to them. I was ready to fight with him and for him. Something I had learned was absent in my behavior with Derrick.

The doctors also told me that there was no set age that the illness surfaces. It didn't mean that both boys wouldn't get it. It simply meant that we needed to be prepared and watch for the signs. So, I did. It was the motherly thing to do. I would do my part to help them manage through the illness and be as supportive as possible. I was also ready to administer tough love if needed. I knew that this would not be an easy road for both of them, but it was a road we would travel together.

As for me, every year I visit Derrick's grave on the anniversary of his death. The letters may have stopped for me, but that didn't mean that I had stopped talking to him. I would share with him all the events surrounding the boys. I would toast to their successes and share their defeats. I kept him in the know about his mother, news I knew he would be proud to hear. I told him that I was opened to loving again. Unfortunately, I had not found anyone who would love me quite the way he had or better. So, I stayed single and appreciated my singlehood. Something I never thought I'd say.

Trust me, I wanted nothing more than to feel the love between a man and a woman. I would have given anything to be held in someone's arms and to dance with until the music stops. The truth was, as the years went by, I stopped looking. I wasn't waiting anymore for some prince on a horse to come sweep me off my feet. I had already had my prince, been swept off my feet, and survived the curse of a wicked witch. I just wanted Derrick. He was always the one. I didn't want to replace him. I just wanted him. So, I lived in peace knowing that one day, maybe not now, could be in the future, I would close my eyes and there he would be waiting to dance with me again. We would be listening to our favorite Brian McKnight song. He would hold me in his arms. I would breathe in his cologne as I held on tight and would continue the dance, we started all these years ago. Only this time, it would be for eternity.

I would wait patiently for that day. Until then, I'll keep smiling, I'll keep living, and I'll remain open to love; just like I had promised I would.

About The Author

Author **A.A. Lewis** is a promising rising star in the Urban Literature world. Her ability to capture the urban culture transcends what we have come to expect from her genre. She is redefining the term urban literature and daring to create stories that resonate with readers everywhere.

Born and raised in Buffalo, N.Y., A.A. Lewis attended the Buffalo Academy For Visual and Performing Arts, which developed and nurtured her creative spirit. Author A.A. Lewis is also co-owner of D & S Publishing, where she enjoys assisting other creatives realize their publishing dream. She currently resides in Michigan, with her husband and two sons. Learn more about Author A.A. Lewis by visiting her website at: WWW.authoraalewis.com